Learning to Live

Kristin Slauter

www.kristinslauter.com

Notes about Learning to Live

While this book is based on actual historical facts related to the history of Colorado in the late 1800's, I have not endeavored to make it completely and utterly accurate. It is a work of fiction and should be viewed as such.

Enos Mills is an actual historical figure very important to the history of Rocky Mountain National Park. I placed him as a character in the story simply for fun, to have my fictional characters interact with an actual person from that time period. Any assumptions made about the possible personality or motives of Mr. Mills in the context of this story should be disregarded, since as already stated above, this is a work of fiction.

Acknowledgments

Wow! Another one completed, and in less than a year. This book was so much fun to write and I thoroughly enjoyed every moment. I want to dedicate this book to my family, Paul, Jordan, and Katie. I love you guys so much, and without your love and support I wouldn't be able to do what I do. Even though none of you have ever read either one of my books, and probably never will, I know you support me wholeheartedly, and that means the world to me!

Cover model photos and author photo by Sandy Powers

www.sandypowers.net

Thank you Sandy for one of the most fun experiences in my life, in helping me bring to life the vision inside my head for my book cover. Your artistry is a gift, and you share it so well. Your beautiful spirit and enthusiasm for what you do is so contagious. I love you, my dear friend!

Graphic design by Aaron Cooper

Landscape cover photos by Aaron Cooper

www.postrockimages.com

Thank you Coop for your amazing creative vision in creating my cover, and making it WAY more amazing than I ever thought was possible. You are truly talented my friend. Next time we hike, I'll at least give it a little thought before I push you off the mountain.

Cover models – Katie Slauter and Saber Dees

Thank you Katie and Saber for lending your stunning good looks to become the faces of my main characters. May your own love story be a lifelong one like Julia and Cash's. I love you both immensely!

Chapter 1

Julia Fitzpatrick pretended to look for something in her train case which sat atop her lap as the additional passengers boarded the train and made their way into her previously empty compartment. She had enjoyed the brief period of solitude in having the compartment all to herself, but upon reaching Denver a great influx of additional passengers caused her to wish even greater than she already did that this trip would end.

Days of train travel from Boston had taken its toll on her and she was tired. For a fleeting moment she wondered if everything she was attempting to do was nothing more than the evidence of her disgust of conforming to society rising to the surface and transforming itself into a complete farce.

In her mind she shook her head and reminded herself why she was doing this. Yes she was headstrong, and yes her parents, especially her mother, was extremely displeased with her decision to move west. Boston wasn't her scene though. As much as she tried to fit in, and be content to live a boring, ordinary life, it simply wasn't happening. She had such a desire, a burning really, to get out and experience the world. She relished the stories she read in news reports of the "wild west," and she longed to be a part of it.

Convincing her parents to actually let her go with their blessing had been challenging. She finally decided that doing mission work would be the best fit for her since she did truly desire to help the people living in remote areas in the mountains, namely in the mining camps she had read about.

"Why can't you be a teacher? Or even a mail-order bride?" Her mother had been nearly beside herself at the prospect of her youngest daughter gallivanting over the countryside, riding a horse, and getting into who knows what kind of predicaments.

"Mother! Honestly! I haven't the faintest desire to be a teacher, and even less desire to be someone's wife. If I'm to be married, I may as well stay in Boston!"

Julia cringed at the memory of that last major confrontation she'd had with her mother before her father came to her aide, and her decision was final. She wasn't choosing to follow in the footsteps of her two older sisters, to marry and be a society wife and mother. Perhaps someday, but not yet. Not until she'd seen the world and all it had to offer. If she could help a few people along the way, then all the better.

She closed her train case and relaxed a bit as she realized the other passengers who had joined her compartment were busy in their affairs and wouldn't be engaging her in idle conversation. She almost laughed at the disdain she felt for her fellow passengers. A fine missionary she would be, when she didn't even want to converse with those around her. She knew if she had a decent night's sleep, and a bath, her outlook would change tremendously. Fortunately she would reach her destination of Lyons, Colorado that day, and for the first time in more days than she cared to think about, she would sleep in an actual bed, instead of a moving train.

She turned her attention to the view outside the window. She could see the mountains clearly now. They were so amazingly beautiful, she couldn't wait till she could stand on solid ground, gaze up at them, and fully take in all that they had to offer. The scenery throughout the trip had been interesting, but crossing the plains had gotten monotonous and she was surprised how close they had to get to Denver before she had actually seen the mountains.

She smiled to herself as the reason for her trip west was renewed within her and caused a spark of excitement in her, just by gazing at those wonderful mountains. She chastised herself for retreating within the walls of her own mind, and purposed to be friendly and available to those around her, starting with her fellow passengers. She was a witness for Jesus after all, and the mission field was anywhere that she went.

Chapter 2

Julia hadn't realized she had nodded off until she heard the conductor announce Lyons as the next stop. This was it, she was nearly to her destination. Her heart pounded with excitement as she looked out the window in anticipation. The trip from Denver to Boulder seemed to drag on. She'd spoken briefly to the other passengers in her compartment, and learned they were all disembarking in Boulder. When they departed she wished them well and ventured outside the train to stretch her legs during the few minutes afforded her to do so.

Very few passengers boarded in Boulder, and Julia once again found herself in an empty compartment. She was grateful, and had leaned her elbow against the windowsill, her chin in her hand, a dreamy look in her eyes, and gazed at the scenery until sleep had overtaken her.

The train was slowing and Julia looked around at her belongings. She could carry her train case, and smaller items, but she would need a porter to assist her with her trunk. Her mother had wanted her to take much more with her than she ultimately did, not understanding how she could possibly get by without everything she owned, but Julia had limited herself to one large trunk, assuring her mother she could send for the remainder of her things once she was settled. If she ever settled, Julia thought to herself. She had told her parents she planned to stay in Lyons, but truth be told, she really had no idea where she planned to end up. In her mind, Lyons would simply be a jumping off point to lands unknown.

For some reason, she was fascinated by all the mining done in the west. Men leaving their families to go and find work, or worse yet, those who would actually take their families with them. Women and children were forced to live in horrible conditions, with no connections to the outside world. Julia's heart went out to them and she had a great desire to be able to minister to these people. She honestly saw herself traveling from place to place and simply helping people meet their needs, whatever they may be. She saw herself doing laundry, weeding a garden, caring for sick children, and then giving people hope in the form of sharing some bible verses with them, or maybe even holding a church service. She wasn't sure what all the future would hold, but she had a heart full of excitement, and couldn't wait to begin *her* life, *her* adventure, not her parent's, or anyone else's.

As the train came to a stop, she summoned a porter for help with her trunk, then as she stepped off the train and onto the platform of the station, she asked him if he might point her in the direction of the nearest hotel.

"I wouldn't know ma'am, I just work for the train."

Julia looked around, a little dismayed, for someone who could possibly help her.

"Why don't you ask him?" The porter nodded toward a telegraph operator with an office at the edge of the platform, as he set her trunk down.

"Thank you." Julia said as she handed him a tip. She looked from her trunk to the telegraph operator, back to her trunk and the departing porter. It wasn't that far. She would keep an eye on her trunk while she talked to the operator. It was far too heavy for anyone to simply make off with it. She approached his open window as she kept one eye on her waiting trunk. There were a few people milling around, but not enough to block her view of the trunk.

"Excuse me," Julia began pleasantly, then paused until she had the attention of the man working at a desk in front of the open window. "I was wondering if you could tell me where I might find the nearest hotel."

The man chuckled. "Well little lady, I'm afraid you left the hotels behind in Boulder. You won't find any hotels here."

"No hotels?" The idea hadn't even crossed Julia's mind that there might not be suitable lodging.

"Oh dear." Julia looked around as if somehow willing a hotel to magically appear.

"Now don't fret yourself. Mrs. Coleman over at the general store will rent ya a room. She runs a sort of boarding house in all those rooms she's got above the store."

Julia was instantly relieved. "Oh thank you!" She glanced at her trunk. "I'm in need of someone to carry my trunk. Do you know of anyone who could help me?"

"Ahhh, let me see." The telegraph operator appeared to be giving it some thought when a young man entered his office through a door behind him carrying a large canvas bag.

"Here's the mail, George." The young man plopped the heavy bag down, then noticed Julia and tipped his cap at her. "Ma'am."

Julia smiled politely then brought her attention back to the telegraph operator who seemed to suddenly have an idea.

"Tommy, you got a minute son? This lady here needs her trunk taken over to Maude's."

Tommy smiled. "Sure I can help you ma'am."

"Thank you so much. I guess I didn't do a very good job of planning ahead. I just assumed all cities had hotels."

George chuckled again. "Cities, yes, but this here's a town." He paused and cocked his head to the side. Where you from little lady?"

"Boston."

Tommy whistled. "We got a big time city lady here."

Julia wasn't sure if they were poking fun at her, or genuinely impressed, but as she looked from one to the other they seemed to have a look of pure kindness about them so Julia relaxed, and was simply thankful that she would indeed have a place to stay and someone to help her get her belongings there.

"What's a little lady from Boston doing all the way out here in Colorado?" George leaned back in his chair, and crossed his arms as if he were ready to take a break from his work and hear an entertaining story.

Julia, who had already picked up her train case, gloves, and travel documents in preparation to follow Tommy to the boarding house, looked at George with a kind smile and said, "I'm here to do mission work."

Tommy spoke up. "Mission work? Like a missionary? Or a preacher? We already got ourselves a church."

Julia smiled at Tommy. "I'm sure you do, and that's good to know. I don't want to take the place of your pastor. In fact, I probably won't be spending much time here. I have a great desire to help those in the mining camps up in the mountains."

"Mining camps?" George seemed taken aback by her response. "Now that ain't no place for a lady. What in the world do you want to go and do a thing like that for?"

It was Julia's turn to be taken aback. "There's a great need there, both of a spiritual and a physical nature. I want to help the families all I can."

"Families?" George cleared his throat and sat back up in his chair. "Lady, there ain't nothing but a bunch of men looking fer trouble up there in them camps."

Between the days of travel, and the uncertainty of the accommodations, and now the questioning of these well-meaning, but increasingly irritating locals, Julia was becoming frustrated and wanted nothing more than this conversation to end and to be on her way.

"Gentlemen I'm sorry, I'm completely worn out from my travels." She looked at Tommy. "Would you be so kind as to show me to the boarding house?" She looked back at George. "I truly thank you for all your assistance, and I would be more than willing to continue this conversation at another time, when I'm not so exhausted. I hope you understand."

George looked more skeptical than apologetic, but did reply to her liking. "Yes, ma'am. You go get rested up."

Julia led the way to her trunk as Tommy followed, and George bent back over his work whispering softly to himself. "Now that one is a fireball. Maybe she does belong in the mining camps.

Chapter 3

Julia struggled to keep up with Tommy, despite the fact that he was carrying the heavy load. Between trying to keep her dress hiked high enough so that it wouldn't drag on the dirt streets, and walking in a zig-zag pattern to avoid the mud puddles scattered along the way, she figured she was taking at least twice as many steps as he was. She snuck glances at the town itself in between keeping an eye out for anything unsightly she wouldn't want to step in. It was about as opposite from Boston as she could ever picture a place. She knew things would be different out west, but until she laid eyes on it for herself, she didn't realize exactly how different they would be. The town pretty much stretched out before them on either side of the street, with varying types of businesses, including a livery, café, and barber shop, as well as a red sandstone schoolhouse, a library, and a church.

Coleman's Mercantile was at the end of the street, and Julia breathed a small sigh of relief upon seeing the sign. Tommy set the heavy trunk down on the wooden boardwalk outside the store.

"Mr. Coleman will take care of the trunk for ya. If that's all ma'am, I need to get back to work."

"Oh yes, of course. Thank you so very much, I greatly appreciate you carrying that heavy thing all this way. She handed him a tip which he graciously accepted."

"Have a good day ma'am, and welcome to Lyons."

Julia pushed against the trunk to scoot it to the edge of the boardwalk, and ensure it wouldn't be blocking anyone's way, then said a quick prayer, believing that it would still be sitting there when she came back. She opened the door of the mercantile and stepped in to a pleasant space filled with everything imaginable for sale. The rich smell of coffee beans greeted her senses, and she noticed a middle-aged woman behind the counter, and a man Julia assumed must be Mr. Coleman, was on a step ladder, rearranging some tins and boxes.

"Howdy ma'am, what can I do for ya?" Mrs. Coleman greeted her with a pleasant smile.

Julia liked her immediately and approached the counter. "You must be Mrs. Coleman?"

"Maude Coleman at yer service. You look plumb worn out."

Julia had to laugh. "I am. I've just arrived from Boston, and I'm in desperate need of accommodations. I was told you rent rooms?"

"Boston huh? What brings you way out here? You with someone, or are you all by yourself?"

Julia was quickly realizing that the pace out west was much slower than what she was accustomed to in Boston. People liked to talk and find out what was going on, she had discovered, whether she felt like talking about it or not. But Maude was friendly, and she would most likely be Julia's closest contact for some time, so she knew she would need to befriend the woman.

She smiled and hoped Maude would be supportive of her plans. "I came out here to be a missionary. I want to serve and help others, and be an encouragement as I share with them the love of Jesus."

"A missionary huh? In town here?" Maude seemed confused by her response, and Julia was certain that very little got past these townspeople. If something new was happening, everyone wanted to know about it.

"Well, my heart lies with those in the mining camps up in the mountains. I hope to use Lyons as a sort of jumping off point."

"Mining camps?" Mr. Coleman who had been silently working on his shelves, but obviously listening up to this point, came down off his step ladder and joined in the conversation.

"Mining camps are hardly a place for a single woman."

"So I've heard." Julia replied with a touch of sarcasm. "I understand that the people working there may not be of the highest moral fiber, but all the more reason to reach out to them."

"How're you planning to get up there to reach them?"

"I'm not exactly sure yet. I simply want to get settled in and rest a bit first before I begin working on all the details."

Mr. Coleman had heard enough of the conversation to satisfy him for the time being, and also had enough information that he could begin sharing what he knew around town.

"Seems pretty foolish to me." He mumbled as he walked off.

"Oh don't mind him." Maude said as she turned and reached for a single key in a grouping of them behind the counter. "Let's get you a room so you can get some rest."

She walked to the end of the counter and opened a door at the far side of the room. "This way."

The door opened up into a hallway and a flight of stairs. Maude began climbing the stairs, and Julia followed.

"The rooms ain't fancy but they're clean and comfortable."

"Oh I'm sure they're wonderful. I can't tell you how thankful I am that you rent rooms. I don't know what I would have done if you didn't. I made the unfortunate mistake of thinking there would be a hotel here."

"Yep, this here ain't Boulder, and it sure ain't Denver. There's real fancy ones there I hear."

Julia nodded, but didn't comment. She had been in many an elegant hotel in Boston, and she doubted Maude's definition of 'fancy' would even come close to the fine furnishings Julia had become accustomed to over the years.

Maude reached the top of the stairs and headed for the first door on the right, which she unlocked with the key. She let Julia enter first, and then proceeded to show her the room.

"Extra blankets and towels are in here." Maude opened an armoire to reveal a variety of linens, and also a space where Julia could hang her clothes.

Julia looked around the room. A large window let in plenty of light. A comfortable looking bed took up most of the space, and aside from the armoire, the only other furniture in the room was a simple nightstand with a wash basin on top and a rocking chair beside the window.

"There's a café down the street where you can get three meals a day. Anything else I can do for ya?"

"Oh, my trunk. It's down on the boardwalk outside the store."

"I'll have Sam bring it up." Maude paused, and looked at Julia as though she were trying to gather more information about her by just studying her features.

"The room looks lovely Maude, I couldn't ask for anything more. I so appreciate your kindness. Thank you very much."

Maude seemed as though she wanted to say more, but gave a sort of sad smile instead as she turned to go. "You let me know if there's anything else you need."

She shut the door behind her, and for the first time in days, Julia finally had complete privacy. She exhaled a wonderful cleansing sigh, and walked over to the window to take in the view, as she removed the hatpins holding her hat in place. Once the hat was gone she worked on letting her long dark brown hair down as well. It felt good to relax and for the time being, not have to think about what her next step would be. She turned from the window and smiled, feeling very happy and content.

She walked around the room, admiring the simple, yet attractive furnishings. The ceramic pitcher and wash basin had delicate pink flowers etched around both their rim and base. The dark wood of the furniture all matched. The bedding was a dusty rose, and Julia smiled at the thought of spending a night tucked comfortably beneath the covers. She sat down in the rocking chair and relaxed her back into the curve of the wood, and began gently rocking. She noticed a large oval mirror trimmed in the same dark wood as the rest of the furniture that she hadn't seen at first.

The room suited her perfectly, and she closed her eyes for a moment as she continued to rock and think about the reality that she was actually here. It had been such a long time in coming what with all the planning, and then the actual trip itself to make it here. She was both amazed, and a little overwhelmed as she realized that the planning and figuring things out was far from over, but in some ways, just beginning.

"Okay Lord, I'm here, and I'm trusting you to show me where to go next." Julia said aloud, then she stood and walked to the window to look out on both the town itself and the red sandstone mountains surrounding it. The town was pleasant enough, but Julia knew that her heart was calling her into the mountains, so the next step would be to see how to make that part of her dream become a reality.

Chapter 4

Sam Coleman took a sip of coffee then leaned back in his seat at the café. "She's one of those high society types. I don't know what she thinks she's gonna accomplish out here. Probably gonna end up getting hurt and running home to mama and daddy."

George the telegraph operator and Frank, the owner of the livery, sat at the table with Sam, eating breakfast.

"Mama and Daddy may come and rescue her first." George waved a telegram he'd pulled from his jacket. "They're already checking on her."

"She really wants to go up to the mining camps?" Frank hadn't met her yet, but was enjoying this conversation immensely. It wasn't every day someone new and interesting came to town. Especially a young lady who was apparently very pretty, from what Sam and George had been saying about her.

"So she says." Sam took another swig of coffee and dove into his plate of eggs and ham that had just been delivered.

George lowered both his head and his voice as he leaned toward the middle of the table. "Here she comes now."

The three men all looked up to see Maude approaching with Julia in tow.

"Well now," Maude began heartily speaking to Julia. "Sam and George you've already met, but I don't think you know Frank, the owner of the livery. This here is Miss Julia Fitzpatrick from Boston."

All three men stayed seated, and Julia was a little shocked at their lack of chivalry, but had to remind herself that this was Colorado and not Boston.

"Pleased to meet you ma'am." Frank said briefly, then returned to his plate of food.

Julia nodded pleasantly at him, then couldn't help but notice the cold reception she was receiving from all three of them.

Maude broke the silence. "Let's sit down." She looked at Julia. "You'll join us won't you?"

Julia was grateful for Maude's hospitality, but she got the feeling the men would have preferred she sat elsewhere.

"Of course, thank you." Julia replied. Once again the men continued to sit and eat, so Julia pulled out her own chair and sat down. She tried to dismiss the chilly reception and do her best to be friendly. She'd had a wonderful night's sleep and feeling well rested, she was excited to see what the day had in store for her.

"Ma'am, I have a telegram for you." George handed Julia the slip of paper.

"Oh, thank you very much." Julia quickly read the note. "It's from my parents. They're checking in to make sure I arrived safely. I suppose I should have wired them yesterday, but I was so tired I wasn't thinking straight."

Maude looked briefly at the men to sense their reaction, then responded. "What do your parents think about you being all this way from home?"

Julia was hesitant to reply. "Oh, it took some convincing, especially on my mother's part, but they know this is something I'm passionate about, so ultimately it was my decision."

"And yer daddy's footin' the bill." Sam wasn't the least bit hesitant to voice his opinion.

Julia was taken aback by his brusqueness. "I'm fortunate that my father sees the value in what I'm doing, and is supportive in every way."

"Well, we'll see how long you last out here." Sam threw back the last of his coffee, and abruptly left.

Maude sighed. "Don't mind him, he's got his own demons to contend with."

"What do you mean?"

"Never mind. Now what are your plans today?"

"I need to send a reply to my parents first of all, then I suppose I should start formulating a plan for my mission work."

George spoke up. "I can send a telegram for you, whenever you're ready."

"That will be fine. Thank you."

"I'll see you shortly." George stood, and Frank excused himself as well, so that Maude and Julia were the only ones left at the table.

"So tell me more about yourself." Maude gave a comforting smile. "Don't let some grumpy old men spoil your morning."

"Have I done something to offend them?"

"No, it's not that. We small town folk get used to seeing the same faces day in and day out. We get set in our ways especially the older we get, and it's difficult to see someone new come in with different ideas is all. They'll come around. So tell me, what's the real reason you left Boston?"

Julia laughed. "You certainly get right to the point."

Maude shrugged. "No sense in playing games as far as I see. Best to be honest and upfront from the get go."

"I guess I can see the logic in that. Unfortunately there's not much to tell. I honestly do want to be a missionary and help others."

"But couldn't you have done that in Boston? Surely there's a whole lot more people in need in a big city than there would be out here."

"I see your point." Julia sighed as she figured out how to best explain herself. "My mother wanted me to follow in the footsteps of my older sisters. She wanted me to marry a man from a good family, and raise a family of my own."

"And you found that..." Maude began.

"Stifling!" Julia laughed. "There's a whole world out there and I wanted to see it for myself. I'm not saying I don't ever want to get married, but I felt my life had already been planned out for me by someone other than myself and I couldn't bear it any longer."

"That's what I figured." Maude smiled, and took a sip of her coffee. "It's gutsy to say the least. More than most ladies would ever do, or even think about doing."

"Do you think it's a foolish notion?"

"What I think doesn't matter. It's your dream, your desire. You do what you think almighty God has called you to do."

"Do you think the men think it's foolish?"

"Now you're talking like someone who would've never made the trip out here in the first place. You've got gumption, and if I'm not mistaken, you've probably got an opinion or two about the way you want to live your life, so you just stick to your guns, hold your head high, and do what you think is best, never mind what anyone else thinks."

"So being honest and upfront about it, everyone thinks I'm crazy, but I shouldn't let that bother me?"

Maude smiled. "You just keep being you, Julia, and the world will be a better place because of it."

Chapter 5

Julia made her way amidst stares from fellow passersby to the telegraph office. She could tell her first order of business after sending her telegram would be to purchase some clothing more suited to this part of the country. She was sticking out like a sore thumb with her extravagantly made dresses from Boston. After that, she hoped to make her way to the livery to see if there was someone she could hire to take her up into the mountains to visit some mining camps. It would have to be someone she felt very comfortable with, as she would have to spend a great deal of time with them. She would be gone days or even weeks at a time, depending on the needs she encountered.

She walked up to George's customer window and smiled pleasantly. "Hello George. I'm ready to send that telegram now. I'm sure my mother is anxiously waiting to hear from me."

"Sure thing ma'am."

George handed her a notepad and pencil on which to compose her message. She thought for a moment, then quickly wrote a message simply stating that she had arrived safely, and had found suitable accommodations. She also let them know that she would send a letter soon, so that they might know all the details of her trip.

"Thank you George." Julia paid him, then began to make her way back to the mercantile to discuss clothing with Maude.

On her way there, she noticed Frank working at the livery, and decided that since she was passing right by, she would take the opportunity to ask him if he knew anyone who could take her up into the mountains. He hadn't said much to her when she had met him at breakfast that morning, but she hoped if she spoke to him one-on-one, that he would be a little more friendly.

"Hello Frank. I was hoping to talk with you for a moment."

Frank dunked the horseshoe he'd been hammering into a bucket of water. He wondered what in the world she would need to talk to him for. Truth be told, she made him a little nervous, and he wasn't really sure why. Maybe because she reminded him of a very strict schoolteacher, even though he never had a teacher as pretty as her in all his years of schooling, which weren't many. Still, school had never been his strong suite, and for whatever reason he felt like she was analyzing him when she talked to him.

"I am in need of transportation up into the mountains."

"You want to buy a horse and wagon?"

"Well, it's more than that really, I wouldn't have the first clue how to drive it. I want to hire someone to accompany me to the mining camps."

"That's a mighty big request. That's a long drive up there."

"Yes, I'm aware of that, and for that reason I would need it to be someone of good moral character."

Frank seemed perplexed for a moment, then caught her meaning. Julia wasn't sure, but it almost looked as though he turned uncomfortably red. Maybe it was simply the heat from the forge.

"I really don't know what to tell ya ma'am. Maybe you should ask the Reverend."

Julia brightened at that suggestion. "That's a very good idea. I would like to meet him anyway. Thank you Frank."

Frank nodded and turned back to his work, glad that he wouldn't have to rack his brain and come up with any other solutions for this newcomer. The sooner she left town the better as far as he was concerned.

Julia thought for a moment. Should she go discuss clothing with Maude or make her way to the church to talk with the Reverend? She definitely wanted to find out what prospects for taking her to the mining camps awaited her, so off to the church she went.

The church was a pleasant building made of stone, with a white picket fence surrounding it. The parsonage was behind the church with a charming flower lined path leading to it, and a white picket fence surrounding its grounds as well. The small front yard had numerous shrubs and flowers adorning it, and Julia spotted the Reverend tending them.

"Good morning Reverend. I was wondering if I might speak with you."

Reverend James Alton was a kind looking man, with thoughtful looking eyes, and the talent for listening. He cared deeply for his congregation, and never hesitated to reach out to those in need.

Julia stepped closer to where he was working in order to introduce herself, but as she noticed the bees buzzing around the numerous blooming flowers, she stopped short and took a step back.

The Reverend smiled and gave a small laugh. "Ahh not to worry miss, let them do their work and they'll leave you alone."

Julia smiled in return, but kept a wary eye on them as she extended her hand toward the Reverend.

"My name is Julia Fitzpatrick. I've just arrived from Boston."

The Reverend removed his work glove, then shook her hand. "Pleased to meet you Miss Julia. That's no small trip coming from Boston. You must be quite exhausted."

"I definitely was yesterday when I got here, but I've had a wonderful night's rest in an actual bed, so I'm doing much better."

"What can I do for you Miss Julia? Are you by yourself or did someone accompany you?"

"No, I'm here by myself. I wanted to come by and introduce myself, and let you know that I came west to be a missionary. I feel drawn to help those in very remote areas of the mountains, such as the mining camps."

The Reverend nodded in approval. "Praise God, I'm happy to see someone fully committed to making a difference in the world and helping those in need."

Julia's heart swelled and instantly the doubts that had been rising within her since arriving in town vanished. A kind word from the Reverend restored her faith in what she was attempting to do, and even though she still questioned her ability to do it, or even how it would come about, she felt a renewed strength and desire to see it come to pass.

"Thank you, you don't know how that lifts my spirit to hear you say that."

"Oh?"

"Yes, let's just say I haven't received the warmest of welcomes since arriving in town, especially when people find out what it is I intend to do."

The Reverend chuckled. "The people in this town are a good sort, they just tend to get set in their ways, and be a touch wary of strangers. They'll come around." He removed his remaining work glove and laid them down on the ground, along with the shovel he'd been using. "So tell me about your plans."

"Well, I'm in need of someone to take me into the mountains. A person of good moral character. I'd pay them for their time, as I'm aware that I may be gone for several days or weeks at a time, depending on the needs I find. I spoke with Frank at the livery, but he suggested I speak with you. Do you know of anyone who would possibly be willing to accompany me?"

"Let me think." The Reverend pushed his hat further back on his head as he wrinkled his brow in deep thought. "I wonder if old Ben would be interested in doing that?"

"Old Ben?" Julia asked questioningly.

"He's an old miner. Lives by himself at the edge of town by the river. Stays active though, he likes to build things. He helped build the church, and the schoolhouse. Hauls stone from the quarry sometimes, builds folks ice houses and whatnot. Very friendly fellow."

"Do you think he'd be interested in helping me?"

"I have a feeling he probably would be, especially if I went with you to ask him."

"Oh that would be wonderful!" Julia exclaimed.

"Tell you what. I haven't been out to his place for a visit in a while. Where are you staying?"

"I'm renting a room from Maude Coleman."

"Ahh yes, of course. Are you free this afternoon?"

"Yes, I am."

"I'll stop by the store at two o'clock, and we can go out to Ben's."

"That will be perfect. Thank you so much, I really appreciate it."

"My pleasure Julia, you let me know if there's anything else I can do for you."

Julia felt tears welling up in her eyes, she was so touched by this man's kindness. She only wished everyone in town would be as pleasant as he was.

"Thank you Reverend. I really needed to meet you today. It has helped me more than you know."

Chapter 6

"You're really going to go up into the mountains to the mining camps?" Caroline Collier and her daughter Lydia ran the dress shop in town, and Maude had asked them to come over and take Julia's measurements. Maude had some essentials in stock at the store, but convinced Julia she should have Caroline and Lydia make her some customized outfits. Julia had agreed, and was being measured up one side and down the other, while they peppered her with questions.

Caroline called off various measurements for Lydia to write down in between her comments about Julia's intentions. Julia kept having flashbacks of being in Boston with her mother and sisters while they offered their opinions about her life as freely as a mountain stream flows when ripe with snowmelt.

"I've never even been up in those mountains, and I don't intend to." Caroline was a very opinionated woman, and made sure everyone knew exactly what her opinion was.

"Aren't you scared to be up there all by yourself?"

"She should be." Caroline chimed in before Julia had a chance to answer.

Julia absolutely hated being around people who had no desire to put themselves in her shoes and see things from her perspective. Even if she actually did try to explain herself they wouldn't stay quiet long enough for her to fully share everything she had in her heart. She clung to the kind words of the Reverend, and knew that sooner or later she actually would be up in the mountains, away from the naysayers, and able to do everything that she wanted. Until then she would simply be kind, patient, and keep her opinions to herself.

"Thank you ladies for taking time out of your day to come over and measure me. I'll be very excited to see what you come up with." Julia smiled politely when they were done.

"Shouldn't take us more than a week for everything you want. I guess if it doesn't work out for you in the mountains, you can still wear them here in town. Don't want to mess up your Boston finery." Caroline looked over the top of her spectacles at Julia's exquisite outfit.

Julia thanked her again, and paid her a hefty deposit, then excused herself and escaped to her room. She closed the door behind her and breathed a huge sigh of relief. Why must everyone have something negative to say about her intentions? If it hadn't been for the Reverend today, Julia might very well have considered simply packing up and going elsewhere, although she had to remind herself that people were the same no matter where she went. There was very little difference between Boston and Lyons in terms of the way people had an interest in her life and either wanting to control it or at least offer their opinion, whether it had been asked for or not.

She made her way over to the window and gazed out on the small, red sandstone mountains surrounding the town. They were mere bumps on the ground compared to the mountains she would see where she was going. Her thoughts swirled within her mind as she looked out the window. Was she doing the right thing? Everyone around her seemed to be doubting what she was attempting to accomplish, and it definitely made her second guess herself. Yes it would be frightening and yes there were several unknowns, but when she left Boston, it was because she wanted to step outside the box that was the only life she'd ever known and do something completely different.

She thought of the Reverend and how he had boosted her hopes that morning. He was the one positive that was keeping her afloat at the moment. She only hoped that her meeting with Ben went well, and that he was as agreeable as the Reverend, because at this point, she could think of no other options.

A soft rapping at her door disrupted her thoughts.

"Come in." She called pleasantly.

Maude entered the room slowly. "I just wanted to make sure you were okay. I know Caroline and Lydia can be a bit mouthy, but that's just their way. They don't mean no harm."

Julia smiled. "I understand, and yes Maude, I'm fine. Thank you for checking."

Maude tugged a corner of the bedspread and smoothed out a wrinkle. "I want you to know I think it's very brave what yer doin' and I'll help you in any way I can."

Julia truly listened to what she was saying and realized that Maude had been very helpful from the beginning. She'd been so focused on the negativity of others that she hadn't really realized just how kind Maude had been.

"That means so much to me Maude. I appreciate everything you've done for me."

"I know Sam and the menfolk haven't really taken to you yet, but they will. Just give 'um time. It's kind of revolutionary what you're doing, especially being a woman and all, and it's kind of hard for them to accept."

"You're a kind soul Maude."

"Oh, I ain't so much."

"No you really are, and it encourages me more than you know."

"Truth be told, I'm kinda jealous of what you're doing, going up into the mountains and all. It sounds mighty adventurous."

Julia brightened at this revelation. "Have you been up in the mountains before?"

"Oh sure. Now mind you it wasn't for no adventure or anything. Got a sister in Allenspark, and Sam's got a brother south of there, so we've been in the area. It sure is pretty."

Julia smiled at Maude, then looked down and started fidgeting with her hands. "Can I entrust you with something Maude?"

Maude sat down on the edge of the bed. "Of course you can."

Julia sighed and looked out the window. "Sometimes I wonder if I'm doing the right thing. I mean, I have this plan, but what if it's not the right one?"

Maude looked at her inquisitively. "Are you the hugging type Miss Julia?"

Julia smiled full on and embraced Maude willingly. "Yes I am, and thank you."

"Sometimes a little confidence is all you need, and I've found that a hug can be just the thing to give you that confidence. Just remember what I told you earlier. You keep on being you. I believe in you and the plans you've got a cooking."

"You don't know how much that means to me. As much as I want to be strongly self-sufficient, doubts seem to find their way into my mind, and it lessens my resolve."

"You'll do just fine Miss Julia. You wouldn't have made it all the way out here if you weren't a strong woman. You just keep believing in yourself, and you'll do fine."

Julia hugged Maude again. "I'm so thankful I met you. You've definitely been a bright light since I got here."

"I'm thankful I met you too Julia. What this world needs is more people like you, who aren't afraid to go against the grain."

"Well I've definitely perfected that, now I just have to see if I can make a lasting difference of some kind."

"Oh you will. I have no doubt."

Chapter 7

Julia was on the boardwalk outside the mercantile a few minutes before two. She was excited to meet this Ben character, and hoped he would be willing to accompany her. She also hoped she would get along with him, since if he did agree to drive her, they would be spending a great deal of time together.

The Reverend arrived presently, driving a wagon pulled by two beautiful horses. Julia was surprised to see him in a wagon, she figured they would just walk.

"Hello Miss Julia." The Reverend tipped his hat, then quickly got out of the wagon in order to assist Julia up into it.

"I thought he lived in town?" Julia questioned as she settled herself on the wagon seat.

"At the edge of town. It isn't far, but I thought it might be a bit much of a walk for a lady since our streets aren't the smoothest or cleanest in the world."

Julia smiled at his thoughtfulness. "Thank you so much. I hope it wasn't any trouble getting your horses hooked up to the wagon."

"None whatsoever. They don't get a whole lot of exercise, so they enjoy getting out whenever I let them."

"They're beautiful horses." Julia watched their flowing manes as they pulled the wagon with ease."

"I've had them three years. Bought them as a pair, so they get along quite well with each other."

Already they'd gone down a couple of side streets that Julia had never seen before. She was surprised that there appeared to be more to this town than at first she realized. The businesses were all on the main street, but they were passing multiple homes now.

The last house at the edge of town before the dirt road ended, emerged and the Reverend pulled the horses over and tied them to a large shady tree in front.

"This is Ben's house. He's probably out back doing something down by the river, but we'll knock on his door first."

The Reverend helped Julia down and she took in the surroundings. It was a pleasant enough property, right by the river with a smallish house and what appeared to be a barn or shed of sorts that was just as big as the house, off to one side.

It was apparent that someone had lived here quite a while. There were several personalized touches outside the house, such as a wooden swing hanging from one of the large trees, and a fenced off garden area. There were several items scattered around between the house and the barn – a wheelbarrow, a pile of stones, some type of rusty old equipment Julia thought might have been a plow. It was obvious Ben liked to tinker, and he kept himself quite busy.

The Reverend knocked on the door, but when there was no answer, he suggested they work their way around the back.

Julia was amazed at the beauty of the river flowing quietly by the back of the property. How pretty and serene it must be to live here. Julia knew if she ever lived by a river, she would spend a great deal of time sitting by it, and enjoying the sound of the moving water.

"Howdy Reverend."

Julia looked toward the sound of the voice to see a little old man with gray hair and a neatly trimmed beard. He appeared to have been fishing, although it didn't look like he had caught anything.

"Hello Ben, how are you doing today?"

"Pretty good Reverend, just seeing if the fish are biting, and they aren't." Ben laughed at himself, and looked with interest toward Julia. "Who ya got with ya there Reverend?"

"Allow me to introduce Miss Julia Fitzpatrick of Boston."

Ben shook Julia's hand delicately. "Boston eh? Never been to Boston, but I've seen pictures. Mighty impressive buildings there."

"Yes, you could definitely say that." Julia smiled. So far he seemed pleasant enough.

"What brings you out to Colorado?"

The Reverend intervened at this point. "That's what we wanted to talk to you about Ben. Do you have a few minutes?"

"Sure. Let me put this fishing gear away and we can head on up to the house."

Ben disappeared into his workshop, and reappeared a moment later without the fishing pole. The Reverend and Julia stood by the backdoor and Ben invited them in.

Ben's house was simple, a main room which included the kitchen, and two bedrooms off to the side. The main room was filled with handcrafted wooden furniture that Ben had made himself.

"Have a seat. I'll put the kettle on."

"This furniture is beautiful. So intricate, and so many details." Julia ran her hand over the smoothly polished top of a rocking chair that had little carved birds and flowers in its back.

"Ben is quite a craftsman. I don't think there's anything he can't make."

Ben lit the stove and put a kettle on for tea, then joined the two of them and sat down. "Well it's a hobby really. Keeps me busy, and out of trouble." He laughed at himself again and looked at the Reverend and Julia. "So what can I do for ya?"

"Well Ben," The Reverend began, "Julia has come out west to be a missionary. She feels a calling to serve those less fortunate and isolated from people."

Ben nodded as he rocked in another rocking chair across from the one Julia was sitting in. "Good, good. Best work to do is the Lord's work I always say."

"She feels especially strongly about going up into the mountains to the mining camps."

Ben stopped rocking. "Oh?"

Julia spoke up at this point. "Yes, I have done a lot of study back in Boston on life in the mining camps out west. The stories are heart wrenching how people work so hard and have little else in their life other than digging in a mine. Some of them even take their families along and women are so isolated from friends and family as they attempt to care for and raise their children. It touched me deeply, and I had a great desire to come out here and minister to these people any way I could. I want to care for their physical needs, but also their spiritual ones. I realize that there may be camps that are rough in terms of the men living there, but this is something that's definitely in my heart, and I have to believe that there are people who need what I have to offer.

Ben had been listening intently. "You plan on doing this yourself?"

Julia smiled, and prayed a silent prayer that Ben would be receptive. The Reverend took over for her. "She would need someone to go with her. She knows nothing about the terrain, and as she alluded to, it wouldn't be safe for her to be there by herself. I thought you would be a good choice to take her up there. You know the land very well, and you would make sure she made it back alright."

"I would pay you of course for your time. Would this be something you would consider?"

The kettle was whistling, and Ben hopped up to take it off the stove. He came back with a tray and three cups of steaming hot tea which he handed out before sitting back down.

"Young lady, I'd be honored to accompany you, but I insist that whatever you were planning to pay me, you give to the people up in the camps. Maybe not outright money, but buy some supplies to take up there and give to 'um."

"Oh absolutely! Thank you so much sir. I greatly appreciate this."

Ben seemed to not even notice her appreciation, but had a lot to say. "It won't be easy, no sir. Long, rough ride in a wagon – two or three days to get there. Not even sure what we'll find when we do get there."

Julia could tell the wheels in his mind were spinning as he was thinking of things he would need to tell her. He glanced at Julia. "You got any other clothes with ya?"

Julia laughed. "I'm having some made. I'll make sure I'm dressed for the trip."

"I've got all the supplies we'll need for camping out, and I'll let ya know what you should get from the store."

Julia felt Ben seemed excited, and wondered if a part of him wished he was still a miner. There would be plenty of time to talk when they were on their way though, and Julia didn't want to take up too much of his time.

"How soon were you thinking of going?"

"The clothes I'm having made should be done in about a week. Once I have those, and whatever supplies I need to purchase, then I'll be ready whenever you are."

"You got here at just the right time. Winter snows are melted out and we've got several weeks of good weather ahead of us before the snows start up again. As soon as you have what you need little lady, we'll head out."

Julia was ecstatic. She had wondered if her plan would actually pan out, and now all the pieces were falling into place.

"I'm so grateful for your help in this endeavor, Ben. I thank you from the bottom of my heart."

"We got a big journey ahead of us, but it's gonna be worth it little lady. Just you wait and see."

Chapter 8

Julia stood in the Coleman's store going over the list Ben had given her of everything they would need, yet again. She had been marking things off of it once Maude had supplied it, but she was still waiting on a few items that would arrive in a shipment before she and Ben were to depart.

Word had of course gotten around town that Ben would be accompanying her into the mountains, and perhaps it was just her imagination, but Julia felt that the men in town who had seemed so against her being there initially, had softened and shown her just a touch more of civility. Sam had even wished her well in all of her endeavors, which had just about caused her jaw to hit the floor. Of course she knew it all had to do with the fact that Ben was taking her. He was respected in this community, and Julia was thankful that he saw enough value in what she wanted to accomplish that he was willing to be a part of it.

The only cloud hanging on her horizon at the moment was what her parents would think of her plans. If her mother knew that she would be camping out up in the mountains for days on end, she would be beside herself. Her father would be hesitant as well, but Julia knew if he had the opportunity to speak with Ben, he would realize that she would be well taken care of. In the end she had sent them a very long letter, detailing everything about the town of Lyons she could think of. She told them how she especially liked the Reverend, and of Maude's kindness, and of her comfortable accommodations above the store.

As far as what she would be doing, she told them she would be visiting those people living away from town, with the assistance of others from the town church. It was basically the truth, only with certain details left out. She *would* be visiting those that lived away from town, she just left out the detail that they lived up in the mountains in a mining camp. And Ben was a member of the town church and he was assisting her. She felt confident in her choice of what exactly to tell her parents. She loved them and respected their opinions, but this was something she was doing on her own and she didn't want them worrying or trying to talk her out of what she wanted to do. She would send additional letters as soon as she returned to town.

Caroline and Lydia had finished her clothing, and Maude had shown her how to pack things she would need in canvas knapsacks, rather than her heavy trunk. It seemed strange to fold things up and stuff them in a bag rather than lay them out nicely in her trunk, but these dresses were so different from her Boston gowns, that they hardly took up any room compared to them. It was incredibly liberating in a way, and Julia enjoyed the feeling of freedom that accompanied her new way of dressing. She was going into the mountains, not to a ball in Boston, and with her new path down the road of life, she now felt she was dressed for it.

"There's a pretty good chance that shipment will be on todays' train." Maude's voice brought Julia back to the present.

"Oh that would be wonderful Maude. Then we could leave tomorrow instead of the day after."

Julia had been in contact with Ben several times since their first meeting, and they discussed many aspects of their journey. Every day it seemed that Ben came up with something else he thought Julia should bring along. They had been slowly packing the wagon, and were nearly ready to go. They were waiting on a shipment of children's books that Julia had thought would make a wonderful present to any children she encountered along the way. They were full of drawings, so even if the children couldn't read yet, they would still be entertained by looking at the pictures.

"I think you've got everything you could possibly think up to take along and more." Maude had been watching Julia's progress throughout the week with interest and had seen the loads of items she had given to Ben to pack.

"I definitely feel prepared. All that's left now is actually leaving and heading up into the mountains."

"Are you nervous?"

Julia smiled at Maude as she considered her answer thoughtfully. "I'd be lying if I said I wasn't, but I think it's more of a nervous excitement than actually being scared. I'm just ready to get started and see what happens."

Just then Sam came in carrying a crate, with Ben right behind him. "Your books are here."

"Oh that's wonderful!" Julia went toward him to inspect the crate. "These were some of my favorite books as a child."

"Mighty kind of you to be takin' so much to give away." Maude looked over Julia's shoulder at the assortment of books.

"Not sure how many children you'll be encountering." Sam still seemed skeptical, but had definitely softened in his manner toward Julia.

"Well, she'll be ready if we do." Ben grinned at Julia, and she was grateful for his encouragement.

"I guess that's it then." Julia smiled as she realized they finally had everything they had been waiting on. She looked at Ben. "Are you ready to head out tomorrow?"

"Yes indeed. We'll head out at first light."

Julia could barely contain her excitement. Everything had come together beautifully, and tomorrow she would begin the greatest adventure of her life.

Chapter 9

It was still pitch black when Julia rolled out of bed. She didn't feel like she'd slept at all, her mind was too full of thoughts and excitement about what lay ahead. She'd realized it would be her last night in a real bed for a while, but trying to force sleep hadn't worked, so she simply lay there and daydreamed about the people she would meet and the sights she would see.

She dressed quickly and gathered the few items she hadn't already packed that she would keep in her personal knapsack. Taking a final glance around the room that had been her home for this short time, she realized she was ready to go, and took a moment before leaving to offer yet another prayer for wisdom and direction, as well as protection on her journey.

Ben was waiting with the wagon parked right outside the store when she appeared. The early morning air was cool still and the first signs of the pending sunrise were etched across the sky. Julia eagerly climbed into the wagon, a much easier task in her new user friendly clothing, and they were off.

Ben had a great knowledge of the mountains and many years of experiences and adventures in them. Julia provided a new set of ears to listen to all of his stories, which he told, one after the other. Julia was thankful that he liked to talk. It helped pass the time, and she was also very eager to learn all she could about where they would be travelling.

"So you were a miner?" Julia had been wanting to talk with Ben in depth about his experiences in mining. She was hopeful to glean some insight into how miners lived so that she would be better able to understand and help them.

"Yes, ma'am. I was out in California when the gold rush hit. It was way different out there from anything here in Colorado. In the early days you could walk around and pick gold nuggets up right off the ground. After that was gone, folks went to panning for gold out of the streams. More and more people came, and eventually the mining operations became more intricate and required a lot of money to get the operation going."

"It sounds exciting."

"Oh it was a time all right. Lots of greed. Lots of people who couldn't be trusted."

"Did you make a fortune out there?"

Ben laughed. "A fortune, no I wouldn't say that, but I did well enough that by the time things got a lot more complicated, I decided to take what I had, and head to Colorado."

"Why Colorado?"

"I have a sister who lives in Denver. She had just gotten married around that time and had sent me letters asking me to come and work for her husband."

Ben chuckled a moment before continuing. "You see I was always kind of the rebel in our family. When I left our family home in Oregon to go seek my fortune in California, the decision didn't exactly sit well with my mother and sisters."

Julia smiled and thought how familiar that sounded to her own situation.

"Yep my sister who lives in Denver is what you call kind of uppity. You know, nose in the air, unless she's looking down it at someone."

Ben chuckled again. "She thought all my endeavors in California were foolhardy, and once she got married to this wealthy banker guy, she thought it was high time I make something respectable out of myself, so she asked me to come to Denver."

Julia was engrossed in the story and was brimming with curiosity to see if Ben had actually spent time as a banker as well.

"When I got her letter asking me to come, I had already decided it was time to move on, and I knew there was still plenty of wild left to Colorado. I wasn't interested in moving to a big city, but I did fancy the idea of taking what money I had made, and finding something interesting to do."

"Did you move to Denver?"

"No, not really. I moved around a lot back in those days. I would stay in Denver from time to time to visit my sister, but most of the time I was up in the mountains."

"Doing what?"

"Learning about them. Mountains have a lot to teach you, if you'll take the time to listen. I spent a lot of years just moving around, experiencing the wilderness, and learning everything I could about it."

"That sounds wonderful. Did you ever do any more mining?"

"Oh here and there. I checked out the Pikes Peak gold rush in '59, then when things switched over to silver a few years later, I lived in a few camps to see how they were getting it out."

"How did you end up in Lyons?"

"I decided it was time to maybe settle down some place permanent. I still wasn't interested in city living, so out of all the places in Colorado I'd been, I decided living in the foothills would be the best of both worlds. It's close enough to Denver for visiting my sister, and it's right at the edge of the mountains for when I get the urge to go exploring."

Julia smiled. "It seems like the perfect place for you."

"It's home now. I wasn't too keen on Edward Lyon starting the quarry, and actually founding the town. I figured it would get too big for my taste, especially when the railroad came a few years later, but it's stayed small enough and I have to confess I've enjoyed helping out at the quarry from time to time."

Ben cleared his throat, then spoke again. "So how is it that a pretty lady like you travels halfway across the country all by herself?"

Julia exhaled, unsure of how much she actually wanted to share with him. She respected Ben already, but how much would an old mountain man really understand about the Bostonian politics of how well-bred young ladies were to live their lives?

As if reading her mind, he continued on. "It's pretty obvious that you like to do things your own way and all, otherwise you wouldn't a made this trip. I know all about them high-society types from my sister. When she married her

50

husband, it made our mother real proud. She wanted nothing more than for her daughters to marry well, and respectable. I figured maybe that was the case with you, and for whatever reason it didn't sit well with you."

Julia had to smile at his incredible perception, and immediately felt like she would be able to trust him.

"You're a wise man Ben." She laughed a little then began pouring her heart out about the way she grew up to someone other than God for quite possibly the first time in her life. "I wanted out of Boston more than anything. I'm the youngest of three girls, and about as opposite from my two older sisters as one could possibly be."

Ben nodded as if he understood perfectly.

"Mother raised us to be proper young ladies. My sisters never took issue with that. They were always perfectly content to have tea, and make polite conversation, and attend charity events, and go to the opera."

Julia sighed as memories from her childhood came flooding back into her mind. "When I was young, I would think of our social responsibilities as boring. I remember looking out a large picture window in my grandmother's home, at the biggest lilac bush I had ever seen. I so wanted to play under that bush, and pretend it was my house out in the woods. Instead I was chastised for not sitting up properly and paying attention to the violinist performing in my grandmother's parlor."

Julia shook her head at the memory. "When I got older, I wanted to pursue my own interests. I began dreaming of visiting different lands, and being in all kinds of different situations. I wanted to meet new people and see new things."

Ben spoke up at this point. "I take it that didn't sit too well with your mother."

"Not at all. As my sisters grew up, my mother was immediately was on the prowl for finding the 'right' kind of person for them to marry, and by that I mean wealthy, high society, and a good name. They of course had no objection to this, but when the time came that she turned her attentions to me and who I would marry, it was more than I could handle."

"So you left home against her wishes?"

"In a manner of speaking, yes. She certainly doesn't approve of me being out here, but I guess you could say with the help of my father, we came to a sort of understanding. I know she's terribly upset with me, but I simply couldn't bear to have my life planned out and lived for me. My heart wasn't in Boston. I'm not sure it will ever be. Colorado hasn't exactly welcomed me with open arms, but at least I'm making my own decisions, and living a life that makes me happy, which in turn will enable me to hopefully help others to be happy as well."

"Well Miss Julia, I for one am glad you're here. I admire your adventurous spirit, and I think

52

you're going to discover more about life and yourself than you ever thought was possible."

"Thank you Ben, that means so much to me. I can't wait for the adventure to begin!"

Chapter 10

The day passed quickly as Ben and Julia made their way along the road that followed the river, and funneled them into a breathtaking canyon. Julia had spent a lot of time craning her neck upward to see the tops of the canyon walls. It was apparent they were headed into the mountains, since this terrain was much more rugged than the gentle foothills that had led up to Lyons.

When they stopped for meals and rest breaks for the horses, Julia was in awe at the natural beauty that surrounded them. She was finally out in nature, experiencing it with all of her senses, and she found it exhilarating. She had never seen anything like this in Boston, and she wanted to drink in everything she possibly could during this moment in time.

Ben could see how much she was enjoying herself, and was glad. "Just wait till we get to the big mountains Miss Julia. You haven't seen nothing yet. What you're seeing right now doesn't even compare to what you'll see tomorrow.

That evening when they made camp for the night, Julia had never felt more content. She was so full of excitement for what lay ahead, and she was so thankful that she had Ben to accompany her every step of the way. She stretched out on the ground, close to the river, and her gaze was suddenly drawn upward to the darkened sky.

"Oh my goodness, look at all those stars!"

Julia had never seen so many in all her life. The sky was lit up with what looked like a sparkling array of diamonds blanketing every part of it.

Ben enjoyed seeing Julia's response to what he had come to take for granted over the years. "Yep, we're closer to heaven out here in Colorado, so we get a better view of God's handiwork."

"I never thought of it like that. That's a comforting thought." She intertwined her fingers behind her head and rested on her hands as she soaked in the moment. Was it wrong that she felt no pangs of missing home or her family? She felt true peace for what had seemed like a very long time – maybe the first real time in her life.

There was something so blissful about being out here on her own accord, knowing that she herself had solely chosen to be where she was at this exact moment. There were no reservations about what she would encounter from here on out, because she realized wholeheartedly that she was exactly where she wanted to be, doing what she felt in her heart she wanted and needed to do.

"I've never felt such peace. There's something incredibly special about being out here."

"Yes ma'am there is. It's hard to put into words for someone that has never experienced it. It's kind of a thing you have to feel with your own skin and figure out for yourself."

"I think I'm definitely learning. It's like a part of me always knew that this is where I belonged, even when I could never see myself being anywhere except Boston. My heart knew somehow that it belonged in the mountains, and my mind eventually figured it out, and decided to follow."

"That's a special realization to have." Ben sat quietly and whittled absentmindedly in the light from the fire he had made. A cool calmness had engulfed the area where they were, and the only sounds were the running of the river, and an occasional distant coyote howl.

Julia felt a sort of sleepy dreaminess wash over her as she watched the moon rise higher in the sky, over the tops of the canyon walls. "When did you fall in love with the mountains Ben?"

Ben stopped whittling and considered Julia's question. "It's tough to say. I feel like they've been a part of me all my life in one way or another." He laughed. "I guess I was born in love with them."

Julia stifled a yawn, then murmured sleepily. "That's nice."

"Best get some rest Miss Julia. We've got a long day ahead of us if we're going to reach the mining camp before dark tomorrow."

"Yes, you're right." For a brief moment when Ben said the words 'mining camp,' a flutter of nervousness grabbed her heart. Tomorrow would be the opening of an entirely new chapter in her life. She had some preconceived ideas of what she thought it would be like, but no tangible knowledge of what to truly expect. She inhaled deeply and took note of the clear crisp air, accented with the woodsy smell of nature, and decided that whenever she felt nervous, she would remember her first real night in the mountains, and the peace she felt when she gazed up at those millions of stars.

Chapter 11

Cash Parker ran his hand through his sandy brown hair before placing his hat atop his head. Exiting the tent he'd shared with three other men the night before, he stretched and surveyed the mining camp he'd called home for the past three weeks. He couldn't wait to get out of here. Eugenia Mine was a poor example of exactly how well run and profitable a mining operation could be. The quality of the ore being pulled out of the earth wasn't impressive in the least. Cash could tell. He'd been around mining all his life. Growing up in Leadville, he'd been privy to the extreme success that good mining could bring. His family was quite well off, and Cash certainly could have had his place in it. There was something about having his whole life planned out for him though that didn't quite sit well. Kind of like the sorry excuse for coffee that he'd been drinking every morning while at the camp.

He'd made the decision to strike off on his own, make his own fortune, discover his own world. His family was close-knit, and he loved them with everything he had. They were sorry to see him go, but they understood his longing to make his own way in the world, and there would always be room for him at home if he ever wanted to go back.

He appreciated his family more than anything, and sometimes he missed them greatly. The two months he'd been away from home had been strange at first, but he had settled into a routine as he found mining jobs, that eventually led him quite a ways from home, but still in the grandeur of the Rocky Mountains. As long as he was in the mountains of Colorado, home would be wherever he could gaze at the majestic peaks, and feel the hand of God upon him when he did.

It hadn't been easy though. The mining camps were so much more primitive and less organized than what he was used to, and this latest one in the shadow of majestic Longs Peak had been the worst. The caliber of men working the mine would have shocked his parents. These were some of the orneriest men he'd ever been around. They spent their days pounding away at the rock, each hoping somehow that they could find a secret stash of silver or gold and somehow make off with a few nuggets before the mining company they worked for found out. They spent their evenings drinking and cussing it up, each one trying to outdo the other in all their various tales of unsavory exploits they'd supposedly taken part in. Add to that the card playing, arm wrestling, and spike driving competitions, and fights were always breaking out. Cash could definitely hold his own though. He was no stranger to manual labor, and his strong, muscular body showed it. He was young and good looking, but he was hard working, intelligent, and street smart, and everyone knew it. He knew a lot of the men thought he was somehow related to the mine owner, which he wasn't, but he wasn't about to deny it, especially when it gave him an upper hand, and caused the men to pretty much leave him alone.

He had developed a good relationship with the foreman, who had given him the heads up that the mining company on the other side of the Continental Divide over in Lulu City was in desperate need of experienced miners, and with his background, knowledge, and work ethic, he could probably land a job as a foreman himself. Cash had one week left on his contract here at Eugenia, then his plan was to head for Lulu City, since it had become a boomtown, and had actual families living in it as opposed to the ruffians he'd dealt with in this shanty camp. He was counting down the days, but even still, the mere fact that he was out on his own, away from the cushiness of home, brought him satisfaction, even amidst the less than savory characters he was spending his time with.

Julia and Ben had gotten an early start, packing up camp before the first rays of the sun made their way over the horizon. It was a horizon they couldn't even see, but had to trust it was there, since they continued on following the river through the steeply walled canyon.

"We'll climb out of the canyon early this afternoon, and wait till you see what will be waiting for you."

Julia was brimming with excitement at the thought of seeing these truly majestic mountains Ben had been talking about. She had been astounded by the mountains she had seen in the distance as she traveled through Denver, and she was enthralled by the foothills she had encountered as she made her way from Boulder to Lyons, but Ben had told her that she hadn't seen anything yet, so she let the giddy anticipation build as the dream of standing right amongst these towering giants came ever closer to becoming reality.

Ben cleared his throat, then began to speak using a tone Julia had not heard him use before, so she listened closely.

"I guess now is as good a time as any to tell you that the hesitancy of the men in town accepting what you're doing isn't totally something to be brushed off."

Ben's statement caught Julia off guard, and she felt a moment of confusion as she replied.

"What do you mean?"

"Well, I didn't want to discourage you before we left, because I totally believe in what you're doing, but mining camps can be a really rough place for ladies."

"How so?"

"Let's just say that not every man working there is of upright moral character."

Julia gave that a moment to sink in. "But surely there are families, other women, that I would be giving my attention to."

"Let's hope so. It's difficult to say exactly what we'll encounter. The population in those places changes all the time. People move on and new people move in. I truly hope you find people with the needs you want to meet, and they are receptive to what you're doing."

They rode in silence for a few moments as Julia thought over Ben's comments. Of course she had considered the possibility that she might encounter resistance to what she was attempting to do. She wasn't that naïve that she expected everyone to welcome her with open arms. The brief time she had spent in Lyons had proven that fact quite effectively.

She felt Ben had some purpose in bringing this up, other than just as a gesture of goodwill, so she pressed him on it.

"What do you think we should do?"

"I don't mean no disrespect Miss Julia, but the fact is that you're a very attractive, unmarried woman out in the unruly, untamed west. I think to be on the safe side, we should tell anyone we meet up with that you are my daughter."

"Your daughter? You think that's entirely necessary? I mean, not that I wouldn't be proud to be your daughter, but that seems a bit extreme don't you think?"

"I'm not telling you what to do. You're a grown woman with no doubt a very strong mind of her own, but I also know what men can be like in these parts, and it's not a pretty sight sometimes."

"You make them sound like barbarians."

"Yes ma'am, in some instances they can be."

Julia shuddered a bit at that revelation, and decided to let Ben make the decisions as far as that was concerned.

"Alright Ben. I trust you, and I'll let you take the lead on this issue. I must say though, I'm honestly hoping that we encounter some families, some women and children, in need of encouraging."

"That is my hope as well Miss Julia. I can tell you have a heart of gold, and a lot to offer folks. I hope you get the chance to do that."

Chapter 12

The rest of the morning passed quickly as Julia spent time inside her head wondering exactly what they would encounter. She prayed that God would use her to meet the needs of the people they would come in contact with, both physically and spiritually. Ben's concerns hadn't really dampened her spirits, just given her another perspective in which to look at things, and think about the best way to handle whatever situations they would come up against.

They stopped for lunch, and Julia could tell they had gained quite a bit of elevation. They had been rising out of the canyon for quite some time, and she was excited to see the first glimpses of the big mountains Ben kept talking about.

Around mid-afternoon when the rhythmic movement of the horses pulling the wagon was about to lull her to sleep, Ben's voice immediately brought her to attention.

"This is it Miss Julia, take a gander over there."

Julia looked to see where Ben was pointing and gasped in amazement at what she saw. It was a massive mountain that seemed to stretch on forever, both up to the sky and from side to side.

"It's so big!" Julia sat in stunned amazement while Ben chuckled and enjoyed her reaction.

"That's Mt. Meeker. She's pretty nice to look at."

"Oh yes! I had no idea something in nature could be so grand."

"You should see the view from the top."

"The top? What? How do you get up there?"

"You climb it."

"Climb it." Julia breathed out the words in utter astonishment. It had never occurred to her that anyone could actually climb mountains.

"Have you climbed a lot of mountains?"

Ben smiled. "Oh I guess you could say I have."

He had a twinkle in his eye that Julia had never seen before, and she suddenly realized that these mountains held a special place in Ben's heart. Perhaps that was part of the reason he had been so willing to accompany her, because he knew what beautiful scenery they would be seeing. At that moment Julia had a revelation. She saw how much these mountains meant to Ben, and she wanted to discover that for herself. It was almost like the mountains held a great treasure, not an earthly treasure, but a spiritual treasure, and she had to find the key to unlock it. She knew that once she did, she would never look at the mountains in the same way again.

When the whistle sounded, signaling the end of the work day, Cash wished he could keep going. It seemed there were far too many hours in the evening to allow for mischief to ensue amongst his fellow miners, and he wanted no part of it. Eugenia Mine was no town, that was for sure, it consisted of nothing more than some tents to house the men, and a larger tent that functioned as a saloon/dining hall where they could congregate during their off hours, eat, and spend their wages on cheap watered down whiskey, and betting on hands of poker.

Cash spent his evenings outside. Summertime in the mountains couldn't be any better. There was a nearby stream he had explored up and down, and he had even climbed some of the smaller mountains close by. Hiking in the woods was comforting to him and reminded him of many hikes he had done at home in Leadville as he was growing up. The outdoors and adventure had always been a part of him and his family, and especially while living at this place, he welcomed the solace it afforded him.

He already had the clear, cool water of the stream on his mind to wash off the grit that coated his skin as he followed the groups of men away from the mine and down the "street" which was lined with the many tents of the camp.

There seemed to be some sort of commotion up ahead, and he noticed a wagon. He thought it was strange because it was the wrong day for the supply wagon, and the wagon bringing the next month's new mining recruits wouldn't be there until the end of the week.

As he walked toward the wagon he shot a look at its passengers and noticed to his surprise that it contained an old man and of all things, a

64

young woman. As he moved closer he noticed that she was very beautiful, and appeared to be what would be termed a proper lady.

"What in the world is she doing here?" He said quietly to himself as he decided to head over and see exactly what was up. This was definitely no place for a lady.

Chapter 13

Driving into the camp Julia was surprised at how primitive it really was. This definitely wasn't a town at all, but a grouping of tents only. They arrived at either the wrong or the exact right time depending on how you looked at it, because it was apparent that these men had just finished work for the day. Julia did kind of hope she could have casually slipped into the camp and made her presence known slowly, a few people at a time, but as it was, it looked like the whole camp noticed their wagon arriving, and were swarming around them trying to figure out who they were. Another disconcerting observation was that Julia did not see a single woman or child among the bunch. They appeared to be all men, and not only that, but men who were very interested in looking at her.

"Let me do the talking." Ben said quietly to her.

Julia murmured her approval, and honestly felt like she wished she had a gun or some kind of weapon on her. The men began crowding around the wagon, whistling and calling out to her.

"Well looky here, we got us a fine filly at our camp."

"Hey there pretty lady, why don't ya come down here and have a drink with me."

"Looks like some good entertainment tonight!"

Julia was appalled at what she was hearing. Had these men no respect for her as a person? Ben quickly spoke up.

"Hello there fellas, I wonder if you could tell us where to find your foreman."

The men seemed to not even hear him, but continued to ogle Julia and taunt her to join them.

"It's been a long time since I seen a lady as perty as you. Why don't you come on down here and spend some time with me."

Julia felt panic begin to overtake her and wondered what in the world she had gotten herself into. She was about ready to tell Ben to simply turn the wagon around and get them out of there, when from the crowd a voice rang out strong and clear.

"It's so good to see you!" Julia looked toward the voice to see who it was. Even the men stopped their catcalls and turned toward the sound.

The most handsome, rugged, yet clean cut looking cowboy Julia had ever seen pushed his way through the crowd, and made his way right up to the wagon.

"You're early. I wasn't looking for you till the end of the week."

Julia looked into the most intriguing, yet gentle green eyes she had ever seen and wondered what in the world he was talking about. She didn't really care at this point though. This man was different from the rest. He was cut from a different cloth and she knew instinctively that she could trust him.

The presence of this man seemed to quiet all the others, and he spoke loud enough for everyone to hear.

"This is my sister, and grandfather, and I'd appreciate it if you would all move on so I could help them get settled."

"Well, well, pretty boy's got himself a pretty sister. Shoulda known." Said a random voice from the crowd, then they grudgingly began to disperse.

"Don't think you're gonna keep her all to yourself now." Said another voice in the crowd as they were walking away, followed by raucous laughter.

The handsome stranger said nothing, but looked stoically after the retreating crowd, then turned his attention to Julia and Ben.

"Name's Cash Parker. You folks didn't exactly pick the best place to visit, so I hope you don't mind my telling them something to get them outta your hair."

"Not at all son. I really appreciate it. I'm mighty grateful you were here."

Julia was on the verge of tears as she quietly, yet emotionally expressed her gratitude. "Thank you so very much. I don't know what we would have done if you weren't here."

"Not a problem ma'am. Now if you don't mind me asking, what are you folks doing out here?"

Ben spoke up. "This here is Miss Julia Fitzpatrick. She's come all the way from Boston to do some missionary work in the mining camps. You can call me Ben. I met up with her and brought her up from Lyons. I was a bit concerned we might have run into a few men like this, but I never would have guessed it would be this bad, otherwise I wouldn't have brought her."

Cash shook his head. "I've been around mining, and mining camps my whole life. This bunch is the worst I've ever seen. They definitely need the Lord alright but, I think it's gonna take a big burly man with a whip, and not a delicate little lady."

Julia was taken aback. There had to be someone here she could minister to. "Where are the women and children?"

Cash laughed. "Uhh, not here, that's for sure. This isn't a mining town, just a camp. There's nothing but a bunch of rough men around here.

The ones that do have wives and families sure didn't bring them."

Julia was stunned. "Do their families ever visit? I brought books and toys and blankets for the children."

Cash adjusted his hat, then rubbed the back of his neck as he spoke. "I just don't know what to tell you. Maybe there have been families in the past, and maybe they'll be some in the future, but there aren't any here right now. No offense ma'am, it's a real Christian thing you're doing and all, but for your own safety I would recommend heading back."

Julia felt totally deflated. "There's got to be someone in need that I can help. I, I've planned this for the longest time and I know I can be of good to someone."

All the feelings of the recent weeks suddenly started boiling up within her. First from her thoughts of wanting to leave Boston and strike out on her own against her mother's wishes, then the chilly reception she received in Lyons upon her arrival, especially when folks heard what her plans were. Now to top it off, the lewd remarks from the men in the camp. She'd had enough disappointment and she was determined to do what she set out to do.

She sat up straight in the wagon, raised her head, and spoke with absolute confidence. "I would like to speak with the foreman about making arrangements for our staying here. I plan on surveying the area, and speaking with the men who do have families close by."

Cash sighed, clearly thinking that she was going to say something else. He had to hand it to her, she had a fire about her that wasn't going to be quenched at the first sign of trouble. She was a woman who spoke her mind, and he had to admit he liked that about her. She was also stunningly beautiful, but that wouldn't help matters much when it came to keeping her safe.

"This isn't a good idea, but alright ma'am." He looked at Ben and gave him instructions. "Let me show you were you can park that horse and wagon, then I'll take you to see him."

Ben hesitated, and looked like he wanted to say something, but changed his mind and simply clicked his tongue to signal the horses to begin following Cash. He knew how important this trip was to Julia, and he didn't want to tell her what to do, but he knew he and Cash would have their hands full keeping her out of the grasp of the dozens of men who had nothing on their mind except having their way with her.

Chapter 14

"Maybe we should head to Estes Park, and you can work out of there." Ben watched Julia as she unpacked some belongings inside the tent they had been offered by the foreman to stay in.

"Estes Park is another town like Lyons, where I would probably be greeted with the same disdain I was in Lyons. I'm not needed in a town. I want to reach the families in the outlying areas that the foreman was talking about. We can use this mining camp as a base, to go out and minister to families during the day, then stay here at night. If there's ever anyone here at the camp that I can help, I can do that as well."

Cash sat just outside the doorway of the tent trying to formulate a plan. This woman wasn't listening to reason, and was living in a fantasy world if she thought that she would be able to come and go as she pleased from the camp without any repercussions. These men were rough and it was only a matter of time before something would happen. The best thing she could do would be to pack up and head straight out of here, but since she had ignored his advice on doing just that, the next best thing would be to keep her out of sight.

Ben stepped out of the tent into the rapidly approaching twilight of the evening. He looked at Cash sitting there, and said simply, "a word with you son." Then walked a few paces away from the tent to be out of earshot of Julia.

Cash stood and followed, taking note of exactly how many steps away from the tent he was headed, as well as the proximity of anyone else around them. Most of the men had made their way into the tent that served the dual purpose of both a mess hall, and a gaming area. After dinner, the poker would begin, and the whiskey would flow. It would be a few hours still before the men became a drunken mob looking for kicks, and he hoped by keeping Julia out of their sight, that the whiskey, despite making them even more boisterous than when they were sober, would also help them to forget she was even there.

Ben turned to look into Cash's eyes, as concern clouded his. "This place didn't used to be that bad. I remember it being much quieter, and even a few womenfolk and children around. Sure it's a mining camp, and there's always a few bad seeds in every bunch, but you're worried about her, I can tell. I would never have brought her if I thought for a second that she would be in actual danger. I need to know honestly what you think about this whole situation."

Cash drew a deep breath, and chose his words carefully. "We have to get her out of here. It's not a matter of if someone will try to harm her, but when. I understand her wanting to help people and minister to them, but this just isn't the place for it. These men will never think of her as anything else other than a…" His voice trailed off, "Well, you understand what I mean."

"Where do you think we should go? I tried to talk her in Estes Park, but she's dead set against working out of a town."

"There's a small ranch up the valley that's real close by. Nice family. I've spoken to them once or twice. We could see if they would agree to putting her up for a while, while she visits families in the area."

Ben nodded thoughtfully. "It's worth a shot. The key is just going to be convincing her that it's actually dangerous for her to stay here."

Cash agreed. "If you're going to stay here for at least a few minutes, I think I'll stick my nose in the main tent and see how raucous the men are getting tonight."

"Happy to. I'll sit right here." Ben parked himself outside the tent.

Cash wasn't totally comfortable with leaving Ben in charge. He was quite elderly, and wouldn't even begin to be able to fend anyone off, should there be an altercation, but he also knew he needed to go get a read on the general state of mind of the camp that evening. He would go quickly, and try to avoid being seen by others as much as possible.

He crossed to the other side of the street, and stayed close to the tents, which would keep him engulfed in shadow. He was nearly to his destination when the foreman stepped into his path suddenly, and he nearly bumped into him.

"Cash, word is these people staying here are your relatives?"

Cash was taken aback by both the suddenness of his appearance, and the directness of his question. He quickly searched his mind for the best possible response. He trusted this man, at least he had thus far since he'd been in the camp. He had talked to him a little of his family back in Leadville, and knew that the story of

Julia being his sister, and Ben being his grandfather, was probably confusing him.

"Not exactly. I was just concerned for the lady's well-being. You know as well as I do how rough these men can get, and I just didn't want any problems."

The foreman nodded his head thoughtfully. "Understood. Although the way she practically forced me to come up with accommodations for her and the old man, I think she's a lot tougher than she looks."

"Possibly. Or just more pig-headed. I'm trying to avoid any altercations for as long as possible. I wanted to check things out." Cash nodded in the direction he was heading. "Excuse me won't you?" He didn't wait for an answer as he continued on to the tent.

Inside the smell of cigar smoke nearly knocked him over, but he moved quickly and discreetly to the shadows up against the wall. Poker was in full swing, but the men seemed to be keeping things to a dull roar. Cash kept a roving eye, scanning over the room looking for anyone who might be looking for trouble. Suddenly he caught a bit of conversation that made his blood to turn ice.

"Don't be gettin' all worked up like Henderson did. The night is young, don't you leave too."

Instantly Cash's eyes were locked onto the man who made spoken. Harvey Henderson was one of the roughest, meanest men Cash had ever met. He glanced quickly around the room and noticed that Henderson was not there. He wanted to go up to the man who had just revealed that information, grab him by the lapels, and demand to know where Henderson had gone. He knew better. Starting a ruckus would only escalate the situation to a point where danger for Julia would be imminent. He quickly changed directions and headed for the door, but not before someone seated at the table closest to the door spotted him and called out.

"Hey pretty boy, how's your sister?"

Cash didn't pause a beat, but quickened his pace, and broke into an all-out run as soon as he was outside of the tent. He hadn't lost more than a couple of minutes of time, but even that was more than enough for someone like Henderson to stir up trouble. He paused briefly in the middle of the street to listen and look around furtively, yet saw no one. He set off again, in the direction of Julia's tent, hoping beyond hope that Henderson had simply decided to sleep it off after his loss. Deep down he knew better though, and he began running again. He was nearly to Julia's tent when the sound of her scream practically brought him to his knees. His worst nightmare had just come true.

Chapter 15

Julia placed the last of her items that she wanted to unpack on the rough-hewn table that served as the only piece of furniture in the room. The accommodations were about as meager as they could possibly be. She guessed it was better than sleeping under a tree outside, but her mind went back to the previous night, sleeping under the stars along the river. There was something so magical about it, and for a moment she paused in what she was doing and thought about what it would be like sleep under them every night. She quickly resumed her actions though, and shook her head. If her mother knew her thoughts right now she would be mortified. She had experienced so much since arriving in Colorado, more than she ever imagined she would experience when she was back in Boston, but she also knew that she hadn't seen anything yet. This was the frontier, the untamed west, and there was no telling what all she would encounter in the days and weeks to come.

She was suddenly aware of a noise outside the tent. The heavy canvas definitely muffled anything that happened on the other side of the wall, but there was an undeniable scuffling, almost like someone was struggling or bumping into something. The last she knew, Ben was outside talking with Cash, so she moved to the doorway and pulled back the canvas to see what was causing the commotion.

She sucked a breath in quickly in shock and disbelief as she saw Ben being assaulted before her very eyes. Three men had ahold of him. One had his hand clasped securely over Ben's mouth to prevent him from yelling for help, another had his arms pinned back tightly behind him, leaving him essentially defenseless, as a large burly, bearded man was delivering blow after blow to Ben's aging body that wasn't nearly as strong as it had been in year's past.

Without realizing either the gravity of the situation, or the possible repercussions, Julia yelled out for the men to stop. Her voice caused the burly man to stop immediately and turn his attentions to her instead. He gave a sort of half grunt, half gesture to his companions, who proceeded to drag Ben off into the shadows of the night. He spat a stream of tobacco juice, then took a step towards her. In that moment Julia realized what was happening and screamed loudly as she tried to back her way into the tent, away from this horrible man.

The next seconds were a blur as he pulled out a knife and held it against her throat, then pushed her down onto the makeshift bed she had finished making just moments before. The next thing she knew he was on top of her, his rancid breath being exhaled heavily in her face as he threatened her very life.

"You keep quiet or I'll slit your throat."

Julia struggled to free herself from his grip, but the weight of his body kept her firmly pinned in place.

"Don't you struggle none either!" He threatened, as he waved the knife in front of her nose.

Julia briefly went limp in response to the sharp blade of the knife so close to her. Sheer terror had overtaken her, and she willed her mind to think rationally despite the urge to simply shriek and writhe and try to get away from this foul human being.

Henderson took advantage of her momentary lack of struggle, and used his knife to begin slitting the front of her dress.

"That's right. You just lay there, and this will all be over soon."

Full blown panic washed over Julia as she realized exactly what his intentions were. This couldn't be happening. Despite the danger of the knife, Julia knew she had to try and get away. She began struggling again, and trying to kick her legs the best she could, but it was futile since he had his weight on her, keeping her pinned down. She tried to free one of her arms that he had raised over her head, and held firmly in place by her wrists with one of his hands. He fumbled with the knife, trying to rip her heavy clothing, and she chose to scream again, no matter what the consequence.

Suddenly, behind her a figure burst through the doorway of the tent, and just as quickly as she had been pinned down by this odious man, he was being pulled off of her by another. Her first thought was that it was another one of the men who had been attacking Ben. When he was hurled off of her, the knife went thudding to the floor, and her focus was immediately on it. She sprang into action, grabbed the knife, and rolled over quickly to get to her feet. She knew in that moment that she would stab someone if she had to.

There was no one there. Whoever had gotten that man off of her had dragged him out the doorway of the tent. She clutched the knife with all the strength she had in her hands. She hesitated to go to the doorway for fear of what she might see. She heard punches being thrown and a sound of someone hitting the ground hard. She backed her way up to the back wall of the tent and slid down it in terror, still gripping the knife.

The next thing she knew, the doorway of the tent was flung open, and Cash appeared, out of breath.

"We've got to get out of here now!"

Julia screamed, his abrupt actions causing her to somehow fear another attack.

He was taken aback, then seeing the wild look in her eyes, wasn't sure if she fully comprehended what was happening.

"Julia, it's Cash! You're okay now but we've got to get you and Ben out of here before something else happens."

She was still visibly shaken, but seemed to understand what he was talking about.

"What happened to those men?"

"I knocked Henderson unconscious, and the other two ran off. We've got to leave in case they come back with reinforcements."

Julia nodded her understanding as Cash took her quickly by the hand and pulled her up. He started to guide her out of the tent when she stopped suddenly.

"Wait." She said, and then quickly grabbed her train case which held her money and valuables before he whisked her outside and hustled her a few steps away into the darkness where she saw Ben lying on the ground on his side, softly moaning.

"Oh Ben!" Julia began crying at the sight of him.

"Shhhh, Julia! It's going to be alright. I've got to get Ben in the wagon. You follow me okay? It's down by the livery. We can get out of camp easily from there."

It finally dawned on Julia that they were actually leaving camp, and not coming back."

"What about the supplies?"

"Leave them. They can be replaced."

All the events of the past several minutes finally culminated in Julia's mind, and she had a huge rush of adrenaline take over her body, and she realized that getting out of that camp was the only thing that mattered at that moment.

"Can I help in some way? I could, I could carry his legs."

"It's okay, I've got him."

Cash picked up Ben as gingerly as he could and slung him over his broad shoulder. Ben gave a groan, but said nothing.

"Follow right behind me, and try to be as quiet as possible. Don't stop no matter what you see."

Julia nodded quickly, and Cash turned and set off, Ben in tow. In the distance they could hear boisterous noisy men, and it made Julia shudder.

Cash moved quickly at a slight downhill angle toward the livery which was off of the main road through camp. They passed the back side of tent after tent, and fortunately the noise of the men stayed on the main road, away from where they were headed. More time had passed, and more whiskey had been ingested, so when those two weasels who had been helping Henderson finished spreading the word that Cash had laid him out flat, the men would be sufficiently riled up and come looking for him.

He could see the livery ahead, and there was Ben's wagon, where he had left it. Upon reaching it, he hoisted Ben up into the back, then hopped in the bed of the wagon to drag him more securely into it. Julia climbed in next to Ben and cradled his head in her lap, to make the ride more comfortable for him.

"Let me get the horses, and we'll be on our way."

Cash moved off into the night to retrieve them while Julia tried to speak soothingly to Ben. He had blood dripping from both his brow and his lower lip. Julia looked around in vain for something to wipe it with, but the wagon was completely empty. Cash and Ben had moved all of the supplies into her tent to prevent them from being stolen or vandalized.

Cash quickly returned with the horses, and had just finished hooking them up to the wagon, and tying his own horse to the back, when Julia heard a shout in the distance.

"They know where we are now." Cash said sternly, then jumped up into the wagon seat. "Give me your hand, you're going to have to drive."

"What?" Julia looked around in bewilderment, and wondered if she had heard him correctly.

"They're out for revenge. I'll get on my horse and get them to follow me, while you sneak out on the wagon."

"I can't do that! I've never driven a wagon, or a horse, or anything like that before."

"You're going to start now. Give me your hand."

Julia gently laid Ben's head back down on the wagon bed, and stood up. She reached for Cash's hand and he practically lifted her up to the seat. He settled her in, then handed her the reins and began giving her instructions.

"Just hold the reins like this. The horses know what to do. Head out of camp the way you came, but turn north when you get back to the main road. You turn the horses like this, - he quickly showed her how to pull the reins from side to side. I'll lead these hooligans on a wild goose chase till they get tired of chasing me then I'll meet up with you."

Julia nodded, then turned her head toward the sound of brawling men which was growing closer in the darkness.

"Go!" Cash hissed. He slapped the closest horse on the rump and the wagon started off with a jolt.

"Oh dear Jesus help us!" Julia was petrified as she held the reins the way Cash had showed her, and strained to see into the darkness. She didn't look back, even when she heard shouts and hooves, and she thought maybe even a gunshot. What in the world had she gotten herself into? This scenario was certainly not one she had ever thought would take place.

She talked to the horses the way she had heard Ben do, urging them on. Should she try to go faster? What if the rumbling of the wagon made too much noise, and gave away their location, or what if they got going too fast and tipped over? She thought of Ben being bumped and banged around in the back, and how it was certainly not helping his injuries any. At any minute she expected to see Henderson ride up on his horse and block their way.

"We WILL make it." She said out loud. "Thank you Jesus that you give your angels charge over us, and they protect us."

She heard a moan from Ben, and she included him in her profession of faith. "Thank you Jesus for healing Ben, and easing his pain."

She felt a renewed sense of strength course through her, and even though she knew at some point that all of her emotions would catch up to her and she would have a good cry about all of this, for now she was resolved to get them to safety, and nothing was going to stop her.

"We're going to make it Ben. I promise you. We're going to get out of this, and make it to safety." It was the only thought going through Julia's head at the moment, and she was determined to make sure it happened.

Chapter 16

Cash spent several minutes giving the men from the mining camp the run around, and playing a game of cat and mouse chase with them. He was a far superior horseman to any of them, and between the exertions of working the mine all day, and the effects of the whiskey, eventually they grew tired and gave up.

He then headed north as quickly as he could in hopes of finding Julia and Ben no worse for the wear. Adrenaline still coursed through his body, and he knew it would still for several hours until he had them somewhere safe. Ben was in need of medical attention. Cash racked his brain to think of where he could take him. He told Julia to head north on the main road, because initially he had been thinking they should head for Estes Park. That drive would take a couple of hours though, and Cash was concerned that perhaps Ben might not make it that long. He knew there were a few farmers and ranchers in the vicinity of the base of Twin Sisters Peak, but Ben needed medical attention from a doctor, and as quickly as he could get it.

Suddenly he remembered a discussion he'd heard the foreman of the mining camp have with a peddler who'd come through the first week Cash had been there. He mentioned something about a doctor who had sewed up a cut he had on his finger. He also mentioned that the doctor sure lived in a pretty spot because he had a view of Twin Sisters out one side of his house, Estes Cone out the other, and Longs, Meeker, and Mt. Lady Washington out the front door.

Cash was familiar with all of those mountains, and now he knew exactly where they needed to go. He just had to meet up with Julia and Ben, and he would be able to get them to safety.

Julia was nearing the end of her ability to hold it together. She'd been driving for what seemed like hours. Even the comforting light from the moon and stars overhead, which actually did make it much easier to see where she was going, couldn't comfort her spirit. She was restless, and unsure. She was concerned about Ben, whose occasional moans and groans at least let her know he was still alive, but most of all, her mind was focused on Cash. Where oh where was he? Had he gotten away from those men? What if they'd all captured him and beaten him to death? She was all alone out in the great wild wilderness, with an elderly injured man in desperate need of medical attention and she had no idea where to go for help.

"Lord, you're going to have to tell me where to go, because I have no idea what to do." Julia simply spoke her prayer aloud, because it helped her seem less alone somehow.

She realized she needed to think rationally and not panic. There had to be families that lived in the area who would be willing to help them. Instantly though her mind went back to the horrid face of Henderson leering at her, then throwing himself on top of her, then holding her down, then holding the knife to her throat, then using it to begin ripping her clothes.

"Stop it!" She yelled out. The horses twitched their ears as if they were attempting to understand what she was saying, but they kept plodding along, following the road. Julia was glad Ben was in a state of semi-consciousness, because she knew she was acting absurdly. If only she knew where to go. She felt it would be awhile before she could trust people again, and she didn't want to happen upon a farm, only to discover that people the same caliber of Henderson lived there. Julia shuddered at the thought. Ben had mentioned a town, what was it, Estes Park? Maybe they should head there. Another soft moan from Ben made her think of how desperately he needed medical attention. She had no idea how far away the town was.

"Oh Lord, help!" Julia yelled out again. This time the horses didn't even seem to notice, and she was glad that they had gotten used to her erratic behavior.

Suddenly, Julia thought she heard something in the distance. Was that behind her, or in front? She couldn't exactly tell. She strained her eyes to see farther ahead into the darkness, but could see nothing. She still heard it though. What was that? Kind of a drumming, rhythmic sound. Hoof beats! She finally realized it was coming from behind, and before she knew it, the rider was up upon her and rode up beside. It was Cash, and he didn't appear to be injured in any way.

"Where have you been? Did you get away from those men? Can I please stop driving this thing?"

Julia peppered him with questions, and Cash couldn't help but notice how beautiful she looked in the moonlight, in spite of the fact that she was so obviously distressed. He leaned in and took the reins delicately from her hands.

"Everything is fine now. Whoa there boys." He gave a tug on the reins and brought the wagon to a stop.

Julia gave a huge sigh of relief, then turned her attention to Ben, and climbed in the back of the wagon. "I haven't checked on him since we left. Where are we going to go? We've got to get him some help."

Cash lost no time tying his horse to the back of the wagon so it could follow along, then climbed into the wagon seat and slapped the reins to get the horses moving again. "I remember hearing about a doctor who lived in the area. His homestead should be just up ahead here. We can get Ben the help he needs there."

Julia nodded, and gingerly lifted Ben's head into her lap. "Ben can you hear me? We're going to get you help. Cash is here now and he knows where to go."

Ben didn't respond but Julia could see his chest heaving up and down in labored breathing. His injuries caused Julia to have pangs of guilt. "Oh Ben, I'm so sorry. I should have listened to you. This is all my fault." Her tears dripped down her face and she wiped them away before they dropped onto Ben.

Cash felt terrible for her, as he saw this new, softer side of her emerge. "It will be okay Julia. We'll be there soon. Don't worry."

Chapter 17

After just a few minutes of Cash driving the wagon, a homestead came into view. He sized it up, and based on the location, and the care in which the property had been taken care of, Cash decided this was either the doctor's homestead, or the homestead of someone who would help them.

He pulled right up to the door, hastily put the brake on the wagon, and bounded out of the wagon and up the three steps leading to the porch of the cabin. It wasn't too terribly late yet, and Cash thought he could see the soft light of either a candle or a kerosene lamp from one of the rooms. He knocked with determination, then turned and gave Julia, who was still in the wagon bed with Ben, a reassuring look.

Cash heard a stirring inside the cabin, then a man's voice call out from inside. "Who's there?"

Cash spoke loud enough to be heard through the heavy door. "Sir, my name is Cash Parker. I've been working up at Eugenia Mine, and there was an accident there tonight. I've got an elderly man who was assaulted, and in need of a doctor. I heard a peddler that passed through the camp talk about a doctor who lived in the valley here, and I'm hoping that it's you."

The door opened, and a kind-looking man of about fifty, wearing spectacles and holding a kerosene lamp stood there. A woman that Cash could only assume was his wife, stood huddled behind him, dressed in bedclothes.

"An injured man you say?" The doctor peered into the night beyond Cash, and looked at the wagon parked outside.

"Please sir, are you a doctor?" Julia called out from the wagon. "We need help."

The doctor seemed to comprehend what was happening now, and turned to his wife, handing her the lamp. There was an unspoken understanding between the two of them, as she immediately rushed off to light more lamps, and fetch his doctor's bag. He moved quickly down the steps, reached the wagon, and climbed in next to Julia to assess Ben's condition. He checked his pulse, then noticing Ben's labored efforts to breathe, he turned to Cash. "Let's get him into the house."

Cash lost no time helping the doctor carry Ben into the house, where the doctor's wife had already lit several lamps, and had the dining room table cleared to lay Ben out on for examination. Cash and the doctor placed Ben gently on the table, and the doctor grabbed his stethoscope out of his open bag, that his wife had placed right next to the table. He spoke freely as he worked.

"Name's Dr. Cummings, and this is my wife Sadie. You say this man was assaulted at the mining camp?"

Cash spoke up. "Yes, he was beat up by a couple of miners who were being a lookout while another miner..." Cash looked at Julia and his voice trailed off, not wanting to bring up what had happened.

Sadie noticed the top of Julia's dress was ripped, and put two and two together. "Are you alright dear?"

The floodgates opened as all the emotions from the night washed over Julia like a gigantic wave. She realized she was finally safe, and she was so grateful for the kindness of the Cummings' that she could only nod her head as the tears spilled down her cheeks and a sob tightened in her throat.

Sadie was instantly filled with compassion. "There, there, dear. Why don't you come with me and we'll get you cleaned up."

Julia's concern for Ben overrode any thought she had about her own well-being. "Will he be okay?" She managed to choke out between sobs.

Dr. Cummings spoke pleasantly as he worked. "Judging from his shortness of breath, and the pain he appears to be experiencing in his chest, I'd say he has a pneumothorax, which is a collapsed lung. It was most likely the result of the trauma he suffered by being beaten. The cuts on his face are fairly superficial, and he possibly has a broken rib or two. He'll be very sore for a few days, but he'll be fine."

Julia felt great relief, but extreme guilt at the same time. She began sobbing uncontrollably, and Sadie led her gently from the room, to take care of her in private.

Ben was barely conscious, and let out a moan as Dr. Cummings palpated various parts of his body. He spoke soothingly to him. "The worst is over, although it may not feel like it for a few days. You're in good hands now. I'll give you something for the pain, and to help you sleep.

As Dr. Cummings prepared an injection for Ben, he turned his attention to Cash. "So what's the connection between all of you?"

Cash thought for a moment, then replied. "I guess there isn't one exactly, except for the fact that Julia put herself in harm's way, and I felt compelled to help her out of it. They had just arrived in the mining camp this afternoon. She had her heart set on doing some missionary work, reaching the people in the camp and so forth, but I think she thought there would be actual families and people who wanted what she had to offer, not just a bunch of ornery men with one thing on their mind."

Dr. Cummings lowered his voice. "Was she hurt?"

Cash looked down, thinking back to what he had seen upon entering Julia's tent. "I don't think so. I pulled a man off of her, but he hadn't been in there long."

"That's a terrible shame." Dr. Cummings finished giving Ben the injection, then set about to cleaning the wounds on his face. "Is she from around here?"

"No, she came out here on her own from Boston."

"On her own?" Dr. Cummings raised his brow in surprise, but said nothing else.

"Yes. I haven't known her long enough to understand how that happened, but apparently she made it to Lyons, met up with Ben here, and he agreed to take her."

"Well I have a feeling she'll be needing a few days rest just as much as our good man here. What about you? What's your story?"

Cash had to chuckle. He found the doctor quite refreshing and pleasant to be around. He almost regretted having to tell him that he'd been working in the mines, he guessed out of pride. He didn't want the doctor thinking he came from the same background as the men who had done this to Ben.

"I grew up right outside of Leadville. My family owns a mine there."

"Oh? So how did you happen to be at Eugenia?"

"I guess I wanted to make a name for myself outside of my family. I don't like being handed things. I like to earn them. I also wasn't ready to just settle in at home. I'm young and I guess you could say I wanted a bit of adventure in my life."

Dr. Cummings paused for a moment, and looked right at Cash. "I think you could say you got it."

Cash smiled. "Yeah, I guess so. Just maybe not exactly the kind I was thinking of."

"What will you do now? Head back to Eugenia?"

"I'm not sure. I had less than a week to go on my contract, then I was going to head over to Lulu City on the other side of the divide and look for work there. From what I've heard, it's more of an actual town, and I'm hoping more civilized, with a better run mining operation. Under the circumstances, I think it's probably better if I don't return to Eugenia."

"That's probably for the best." The doctor finished with Ben, and began straightening up. "You're welcome to stay here as long as you need to. This old timer here is definitely going to

93

need a few days to recover before he heads back to Lyons. I'm going to go check on the little lady and see if I need to do anything for her."

Cash thanked the doctor, and wandered out to the front porch after he saw him head towards the bedroom that Sadie had taken Julia to. For the first time in several hours he could finally take stock of his thoughts and think. He knew exactly where his mind was headed though, and that was Julia.

There was just something about her. She was stubborn, and headstrong, and had a million opinions about things, but at the same time when he thought about the fact that she had left home and traveled out here to do something all on her own, he realized they had quite a bit in common. Besides her stubborn qualities though, there was a sweetness about her that tugged at his emotions, and drew him to her. He found her very presence extremely intoxicating, like something he couldn't get enough of. He balled his hands into fists when the vision of Henderson having his way with her popped into his head. He didn't even have to think twice about grabbing the brute and delivering blow after blow with all he had in him. It was at that moment when he delivered the final blow that rendered Henderson unconscious, that he knew he wanted to protect Julia above all else.

He shook his head as he let that thought roll around inside his brain. Where were these thoughts coming from? He barely knew her, yet there was just something about her that captivated him. Well, he had wanted adventure in his life, and this was just that. He looked up to the stars as if searching for a sign, then closed his eyes and simply let the moment, and the feelings wash over him. He had no idea where this would lead, but he did know one thing. He had met Julia Fitzpatrick, and he didn't want to let her go.

Chapter 18

Dr. Cummings rapped lightly on the door of the bedroom Sadie had taken Julia into. Julia had been quite distraught, and had sobbed for several minutes as she fought to relay the events of the evening to Sadie. Aside from the sheer terror she had faced, Julia was also very much aware of the consequences of her adamant decision to stay in the camp. Not only did she put herself in danger, she put Cash and Ben in danger as well, which resulted in the injuries that Ben sustained.

"Dear sweet Ben." Julia had sobbed. "He didn't deserve that. He and Cash were right and I didn't listen to them."

Sadie listened compassionately, and knew in Julia's emotional state, all she needed at the moment was a comforting presence, which Sadie did her best to provide. She had drawn Julia a hot bath, and helped her into a clean set of bedclothes, before settling her into the warm, comfortable bed.

Dr. Cummings entered the room and gently approached Julia, reading Sadie's expression for indicators if there was anything specific he should know before he spoke with her. Sadie's face was one that showed Julia was simply sad and feeling terribly guilty.

Dr. Cummings spoke quietly and pleasantly as he asked Julia if he could give her something to help her sleep, and then asked as delicately as he could if Julia had been hurt in any way by Henderson. It was obvious by the look in Julia's eyes that the question brought back the horrible memory of the evening, but she had cried all the tears she had in her and was beginning to simply feel numb.

"No doctor, thankfully Cash burst into the tent just in time. I don't know what I would have done if he hadn't." Julia let out a long shuddery sigh, then continued. "I would very much like something to help me sleep. It's been an exceedingly trying day, and I...." She trailed off, not really sure what else to say.

"I understand dear. A good night's sleep is just what you need. Things will be clearer in the morning." He handed her a pill and poured a glass of water from the pitcher on the nightstand.

Sadie was finished helping Julia, so she excused herself to see to Cash, and show him his accommodations for the night. Julia managed a small smile after she left and leaned her head back into the pillow, relishing the comfort it provided. "She's such a sweet woman. I really appreciate all her help."

"Yes, we make a pretty good team. She's been by my side for a lot of years. I definitely couldn't do all that I do without her. You get some rest now. The medicine I gave you will help you sleep, and you'll feel better in the morning."

Out in the main room, Sadie checked on Ben, then went looking for Cash. She found him outside on the porch gazing up at the stars. "Beautiful sight isn't it?"

Cash smiled at her then looked back up. "Yes it is. Reminds me of home. I never get tired of looking at them."

"Where's home?"

"Leadville."

"That was a brave thing you did tonight."

Cash dismissed his actions. "Just doing what any decent human being would do. I just wish I could have prevented it in the first place, but Julia's a little, well, I guess you could say headstrong."

Sadie laughed. "She's a woman who knows her mind and that's a good thing."

Cash agreed. "It definitely can be, I just think she needs to realize she's not back in Boston.

She's someplace where rules and civility don't always happen."

Sadie was quiet for a minute, then decided to test the waters a bit to see where Cash's head was at. "She sure is pretty."

"That she is, and that's what had me worried at the camp. Unfortunately a beautiful woman, is a recipe for disaster at a mining camp with nothing but a bunch of rough men around who don't even know what it is to treat a lady with the proper respect she deserves."

"Do you have feelings for her?"

Cash looked at Sadie with surprise by her forwardness, and didn't say anything right away.

Sadie smiled and continued. "Sorry to be so forward, but by the time you get to be my age, you just kind of call it like you see it."

It was as if this woman could read his mind. Cash wasn't ready to talk about it yet though, especially with a total stranger, so he feigned confusion. "You think I have feelings for her? I just met her."

"True, but it only takes a moment for a spark to develop."

Cash raked his hand through his hair, unsure of what to say.

Sadie could sense he was uncomfortable. "I'm sorry, I didn't mean to upset you in any way. I honestly just wanted to tell you I think you're a very noble and upright man, and you and Julia would make a good match." She laughed, then patted him on the arm, as he still stood there speechless. "I'll back off. Let me show you to your room, unless you'd rather stand out here and gaze at the stars, and... think."

He looked at her, unable to totally figure her out, but he had to admire her easy-going way, and the fact that she seemed incredibly perceptive could be a good thing, especially if she thought that perhaps Julia had feelings for him as well.

"Yes, no, I mean, I would appreciate you showing me the accommodations, although I don't want to put you out in any way. I'd be happy to sleep in the barn."

"Oh nonsense. We have a large house so that we can care for people when they pass our way. Plenty of extra rooms. I'm sure Carl will need your help moving Ben to one of them, we don't want him sleeping on the table all night."

"Of course, and thank you, for everything." Cash managed a small shy smile to let her know that her perceptibility was spot on, and he appreciated it. As keenly aware of things as she was, he had no doubt she would pick up on it.

Cash helped Dr. Cummings transport Ben to one of the rooms closest to the main room, then Sadie took him upstairs to a large spacious loft area with two additional bedrooms on either side of it.

"Here you go. Should be everything you need. If you do need anything else just ask."

99

"I can't thank you enough. You and your husband have been absolute lifesavers tonight."

"Don't think anything of it. We're more than glad to help. You get yourself some rest now, and we can talk more in the morning."

With that Sadie left and shut the door behind her, leaving Cash alone with his thoughts once again. He crawled into bed, and realized how absolutely weary he was. The adrenaline he'd been running on for hours now had finally worn off and he craved sleep. His thoughts were focused on Julia as he lay there. What would she do now? He didn't want her dream to be crushed because of what had happened. Ben would need to return home when he was able and fully recover there, but what would Julia do? Cash thought over different scenarios as he began to drift off to sleep. Maybe she could stay here and help Dr. Cummings and Sadie. She could minister to patients, although all of her supplies were gone, so they would have to do something about that. Cash wasn't sure what the answer was, but he decided that night that he would figure out a way to help her all he could. She was too special not to.

Chapter 19

The morning dawned clear and calm, and even before Cash opened his eyes he realized he wasn't at the mining camp. The bed in which he slept was way too comfortable, and there hadn't been the usual snoring from other men interrupting his sleep periodically throughout the night.

In some ways, this was the start of a new chapter in his life, although he wasn't sure exactly how it would turn out yet. As he made his way downstairs, he heard Dr. Cummings in Ben's room, calling out for Sadie to bring him some kind of instrument that Cash had no idea what it was. He sounded fairly serious, so Cash quickened his step and made his way into Ben's room.

"What's happening?"

"The pneumothorax hasn't improved like I thought it would, I'm going to have to remove the build-up of air around his lung."

Cash saw Ben gasping for air. He looked so frail lying on the bed, so pale, and bruises were already beginning to show on his face.

"Is there anything I can do to help?"

"You can hold the chloroform over his nose and mouth when I have it ready. I'll put him to sleep for the procedure, because I have to stick a large needle between his ribs to free the air that's pressing on his lung."

Cash felt a twinge of panic. Medical procedures weren't something he was familiar with, and this sounded serious.

Sadie entered the room with some kind of bottle that appeared to be an antiseptic of some sort, and also a large needle with tubing attached to it.

She laughed when she saw Cash's face. "Don't you worry now, we've done lots worse procedures than this."

"Is he going to be okay?"

"Oh yes, he's a tough one. We've just got to get this excess air out of him that's pushing against his lung, so he can breathe."

Cash marveled at how well they worked together. Sadie was able to anticipate what Dr. Cummings needed, and when. She tipped a bottle of chloroform up and applied some to a clean, folded cloth, which she then passed to Cash.

"Hold this over his nose and mouth until I tell you to take it off."

Cash did as he was told, and watched as Ben's breathing gradually became slower and deeper as Dr. Cummings worked. He was glad he was on the opposite side of the bed from where the needle was inserted, because he wasn't sure he would want to see that.

At last Dr. Cummings pulled out his stethoscope and took a long listen to Ben's lungs. He nodded an approval. "That took care of it. He's breathing much easier now."

"Congratulations. You just assisted with your first medical procedure." Sadie smiled at him.

Cash cleared his throat. "How do you know I don't do stuff like that all the time?"

Sadie laughed. "You were as pale as Ben there for a while, with beads of sweat on your forehead. I just kind of guessed."

Cash wiped his fingers across his forehead, and indeed felt the moisture of perspiration. "Okay, you got me. I'm just glad he's going to be alright."

"He's going to be just fine, don't you worry." Dr. Cummings began straightening up. "I smell something delicious out there Sadie."

"Yep, breakfast is ready whenever you are."

Cash realized he was famished, and he followed Sadie out into the sunny kitchen, where she had the table all set. There was no sign of Julia, and he hesitated to ask about her, since there was no telling what kind of a response his inquiry would evoke from Sadie.

Once again she seemed to read his mind though. "I checked on Julia this morning. Still fast asleep. Between the medication Carl gave her to sleep, and the trauma of yesterday, I'm sure she needs the extra rest."

Sadie poured coffee as Dr. Cummings joined them and they all sat down to the best breakfast Cash had eaten since he left home. Sadie had prepared a big platter of light and fluffy biscuits, to be served with a hearty sausage gravy that smelled so good Cash could feel the saliva forming in his mouth. There were also eggs, bacon, and an assortment of preserves that Cash determined he would have to try on a biscuit or two as well.

"So Cash." Dr. Cummings began. "Do you have a plan for today? Ben will need to stay here and rest for a few days, and I suspect Julia will need at least a day as well."

"I need to talk to Julia, and see what she wants to do. In the meantime, I'd be more than happy to help you with any chores or even repairs that you might need done around here."

Sadie spoke up. "That would be a help. Carl is gone so much of the time visiting patients that things tend to get put on hold around here. I do what I can, I'm pretty handy myself, but the bigger projects have to wait."

"Say no more. Just point me to whatever needs attention and you can consider it done."

"Thank you Cash." Dr. Cummings looked at him with true appreciation. "It's true. My responsibilities often call me away, and I'm not able to help Sadie as much as I'd like.

"Well good deal. Eat plenty of breakfast and then I can get you started on fixing the chicken coop." Sadie plopped another biscuit on his plate. "The cherry preserves in particular are extra good this year." She gave him a wink.

"Happy to do it." Cash was hoping to speak with Julia privately at some point. He needed to know where her mind was at. Maybe it was simply the events of the previous night, but he felt not only a desire to protect her, but also almost a need to help her accomplish whatever plans she had. Would she still want to do missionary work? He was almost one-hundred percent certain that all

104

of her supplies still back at the camp, would have been looted and either stolen or destroyed. The more he thought about things, the more he wanted to speak with her, but he also knew she needed her rest, and he'd promised his help to Sadie. Talking to Julia would unfortunately have to wait.

Chapter 20

Julia could feel sunlight against her eyelids, but wasn't fully awake yet. She rolled over in bed, and for a moment thought she was back in her room in Boston. Why hadn't her maid woken her sooner? As bright as the sunlight felt, she would obviously be late for breakfast. A moment of panic ensued, and Julia snapped her eyelids open. Where was she? This wasn't Boston. She felt so tired and groggy, simply worn out. All at once the previous night's events came rushing back to her, and for a moment she honestly wished she had been back in Boston, late for breakfast or not.

She stretched, and thought about simply lying there and trying to fall back asleep, but curiosity got the better of her. She wondered how Ben was doing, and then my goodness, she should get up and help Sadie. What kind of a houseguest was she to think she should could just stay in bed all day? Reluctantly she pulled back the covers and sat up, but a sudden swirling of her head caused her to stop where she was. Oh my. Why did she feel so awful? She looked around the room and saw that Sadie had laid an attractive floral patterned robe over a chair that sat in the corner of the room. It dawned on Julia she had nothing to wear except the ripped dress she arrived in last night. Oh dear. All of her belongings were back at the mining camp, with the exception of her train case which she was so thankful she had managed to grab on the way out. She at least had some money to replace her things, but there wouldn't be nearly enough to buy all new supplies for mission work.

She sighed, then stood slowly and reached for the robe. She slipped it on, and tied it securely around her waist, then moved to the door, but just before she opened it, the door opened on its own and Sadie's cheerful face entered the room.

"Oh you're up. How did you sleep?"

Julia was taken aback. She couldn't remember the last time someone had asked her how she slept. Sadie was unlike any person she had ever met. She had this amazing way of being friendly, laid-back, and helpful all at the same time. Julia was extremely thankful she was there, and was so glad to see her.

"I slept really well. It was hard to wake up and get out of bed, but I wanted to see how Ben was doing, and I don't want to just lie in bed all day. I also wanted to see if you needed help with anything."

"Oh goodness no. You need rest. I want you to just enjoy your time here, and make yourself at home. If there's anything YOU need help with, I'll be the one doing the helping."

Sadie set about to straightening and fluffing the bed as she continued talking. "Ben is doing well. He's resting comfortably. Carl had to do a procedure on him this morning to help him breathe easier and help his collapsed lung heal faster, but he's doing fine, and when he wakes up I'm sure he'll be glad to see you."

Julia was quiet as Sadie spoke. The guilt she began feeling last night returned when she thought about Ben having to endure a procedure, and no doubt quite a bit of pain accompanied with the injuries he had sustained.

Sadie glanced at her, and knew immediately what she was thinking. "Now don't you fret yourself none. He's going to be fine. He's on medication to ease the pain. He just needs a few days rest and he'll be good as new "

Julia sat down in the chair the robe had been slung over. "You don't understand. Ben wouldn't be in the condition he's in if it wasn't for me. He tried to talk me out of staying in the mining camp, but I wouldn't even listen to him."

Sadie stopped straightening and looked at Julia. "I guarantee you either one of those men would have given their life for you last night. You did what you thought was best at the time. You can't look back with regret. Cash is fine, and Ben will be fine. Don't beat yourself up over it."

At the mention of Cash's name, Julia thought of everything he had done for her as well, and yet she barely knew him.

Sadie saw the change in Julia's demeanor when she talked about Cash, so she took the opportunity to determine how Julia felt about him.

"Cash is a good man. It's obvious he has a real caring heart." Sadie wanted to comment on the fact that he was very handsome as well, but she decided that might be taking things a bit too far considering that Julia still seemed to be pretty emotionally fragile.

Julia seemed to let Sadie's words soak in a moment before she responded.

"Yes. I'm very grateful for all he has done."

Julia shook her head, closed her eyes and squeezed the bridge of her nose, while exhaling heavily.

"What's wrong?"

"I need to talk to him. I need to apologize. It's just that I was so certain that I…" Julia trailed off for a moment then began again. "I wanted to do things the way I wanted to do them without feeling like people were controlling me or telling me what to do. I just picked the wrong people not to listen to."

Sadie wasn't completely sure what all Julia was talking about, but she simply listened anyway and let her express what was inside her. "Go on."

"I don't even know what I'm trying to say. I guess I'm just frustrated."

"Well I know just the cure for that. Come get a cup of tea and sit on the front porch and gaze at the mountains. We've got a marvelous view, and there's just something about taking it all in that makes a person feel better."

Julia smiled, then looked down at the robe hanging from her body. "I have nothing to wear."

"Don't you worry about that. I'll fetch you one of my dresses. Of course it'll be a might big on you, but I'll get yours repaired in no time at all."

"I don't mean to be a bother to you. I don't want to keep you from doing what you need to do."

"Nonsense. Now that I've put Cash to work, he'll put me way ahead on all my projects."

"You put Cash to work?"

"Yep, he's out mending the chicken coop right now. Let me get you that dress."

Sadie left the room and Julia walked over to the window to look outside. She spotted the chicken coop, and there was Cash, working away. She tried to process everything that had happened since the previous day. She had gone from arriving at a mining camp with the hope of doing mission work, to staying in a stranger's house, wearing another woman's clothes, and not knowing what in the world she would be doing next. On top of that, Ben lay in a bed, recovering from injuries and Cash was doing chores. Oh

109

dear, had she lost him his job at the mining camp too? Julia fought the urge to run outside in her nightclothes and beg for his forgiveness. She was so racked with guilt, she could barely stand it.

Sadie returned with the dress, and announced that Ben was awake.

"Oh good. Do you think I could speak with him?"

"Of course. Now don't you fret about anything. Everything is going to be just fine. You get dressed, and I'll fix you that tea."

Julia quickly changed and folded the nightgown and robe neatly on the bed, then opened the bedroom door and ventured outside. In her state last night she hadn't really gotten the lay of the house. To her right there was a staircase leading up to another level, and a door at the end of the hallway that she assumed must be Sadie's and Dr. Cummings bedroom. Across the hall from her room was another door that was open so she peeked in and saw Ben lying in bed, propped up on several pillows. His face was quite bruised which made her want to gasp, but she managed to hold it in as she smiled and walked toward him as he noticed her.

"Ben it's so good to see you awake."

She grasped his hand gently, and as much as she didn't want to, the tears began to well up in her eyes.

"Now none of that Miss Julia." He said quietly. "I'm sure I'm a sight to look at, but there's no need for tears."

"I feel so awful about all of this. I'm so sorry I didn't listen to you. If we had left right away none of this would have happened."

"Don't you worry one bit about that. It's over now. We'll just have to come up with a different plan."

Julia nearly burst into tears at the kindness of this sweet man. Even as he lay there injured, he was still thinking of her and her plans, which in her mind didn't even exist anymore. She had no idea what she was going to do next, but she was done involving others when there was the potential for danger.

"Thank you Ben. I really appreciate all you have done for me. I couldn't imagine a more wonderful person to spend time with, and I will truly cherish the moments we had together."

"That sounds like you're saying goodbye."

"I guess maybe I am. As soon as Dr. Cummings says you can travel I want you to go back to Lyons. I regret so deeply putting you in danger, and while I'm not sure where to go from here, I don't want to subject you to any more of my whims."

"Now Miss Julia, you're thinking too emotionally, and I would hardly call what you set out to do a whim. Let's not decide anything right now." Ben coughed, and winced in pain. "We'll know what to do when the time is right."

Julia cringed to see him suffer, but was also grateful for his wisdom. "Just rest Ben, and we'll talk more later."

Ben nodded and closed his eyes, so Julia left and made her way into the kitchen where Sadie was pouring her a cup of tea.

"You take this, and you go sit a spell on the porch. Quit beating yourself up over what happened, and be thankful everything turned out as well as it did."

Julia had to smile at Sadie's directness. She was one of the most interesting people she had ever met. She got right to the point, and Julia could tell she liked to fix things, whether it be chicken coops or people's hearts, and she liked that immensely about her.

Julia took the tea and walked out to the porch. The air was pleasantly cool but not too cold, and smelled so fresh that it relaxed her immediately. She sat down in one of the many wooden hewn chairs adorning the porch, and took a look around. The property was very pleasant, and had an open meadowy feel to it, with a few trees here and there scattered on the lawn, leading up to thick forest surrounding it. The mountain views were indeed incredible, and she could see how therapeutic it would be to live in this peaceful environment.

"Be thankful everything turned out as well as it did." Sadie's words echoed in Julia's mind as she sipped her tea. What did she have to be thankful for? Well first of all, they were all alive, and Ben was going to recover. Cash had gotten them out of that horrible place, and rescued her from the grips of that awful man before anything permanently scarring had taken place. She was thankful for all those things, but what now? Her resources were gone, she didn't have enough money left to replace them, and if she was truly honest with herself, so was the desire to even try to help others. What was she doing here anyway? A well-bred Boston girl trying to help those living in the west? She was the one who needed the help. She was completely out of place here. No wonder everyone in Lyons had thought she was crazy for doing this. She *was* crazy. It was a crazy, stupid idea, and she felt like she had completely and utterly failed.

She sighed, and if she had any tears left to cry she would have, but none seemed to come. She looked up at the three giant mountains she saw right in front of her. They stood there so regally against the bluest sky Julia had ever seen. Her thoughts went back to the night she and Ben had spent along the river. She had felt such peace and contentment that night, but as she searched her heart for what her exact feelings had been, she realized that it wasn't so much that she was there to help others, but just the fact that she was there. She was in the mountains, and she had broken free of the confines of her life in Boston. As she thought about her feelings, she realized that while perhaps she had failed at ministering to others, these mountains were ministering to her, and maybe that was what she needed most of all.

She wondered if Cash would insist on her returning to Lyons with Ben when he was able. Well she wasn't going to. There was more for her to discover out here, she felt it within her, and she would do it on her own if she had to. She would start by sending a telegram to her parents. They would be anxious to hear from her, but what in the world should she tell them? If her parents knew the truth, her mother would probably send her father out to bring her home immediately. That was the last thing she wanted. She would have to tell them portions of the truth like she had previously, and simply leave it at that. Then she had to have at least some new articles of clothing since after last night, she was left with absolutely nothing.

She thought about talking to Cash, but decided against it. She did want to thank him for his actions last night, and apologize for the entire situation, but she was also hesitant because she was convinced that he would try to get her to go back to Lyons, or worse yet, even back to Boston. She was about to go inside and talk to Sadie, when the front door opened, and she appeared on the porch.

"Feeling better?" Sadie had her own cup of tea, and sat down next to Julia.

"A little yes."

Sadie took a sip as she looked at Julia over the rim of her cup. She swallowed, then spoke. "You've got a look in your eye."

Julia looked confused. "What do you mean?"

"I mean, I think you've been out here hatching a plan. Am I right?"

Julia shrugged and kind of shook her head. "Oh, I don't know. I know I don't want to go home or back to Lyons, that's for sure."

"Who said anything about that?"

"No one I guess. I just assumed that Cash would probably think it was best if I went back with Ben whenever he's ready to travel."

"Is that what you want to do?"

"No, it isn't."

Sadie didn't say a word, but waited for Julia to elaborate.

"I'm not really sure what I want to do, or where I'll go from here, but I guarantee you my adventure is far from over."

"I wouldn't expect any less from you."

"How can you say that? You barely know me."

Sadie took another sip of her tea. "I know enough. The simple fact that you came all the way out here from Boston on your own tells me that you've got more determination than most every other woman around. Even the ones who live out here."

"I used to think so. Either it was determination or just longing so badly for a different set of circumstances than the ones I was living in."

"Well that's determination. You made it happen didn't you?"

"I guess so."

"What do you mean, you guess so? You did. Now you've had a little setback, but don't let that stop you from doing what's on your heart to do."

Julia sat up straighter at that comment. "That's just it. I'm not even sure what I want to do anymore. After last night, I'm totally deflated, but not just because I have to collect my thoughts, gather more supplies, and start over. I don't even think I want to try again. I suddenly have no desire to try and help others." Julia put her hand over her mouth when she realized what she had said. "That sounded terrible, I, I didn't mean it like that."

"Of course not." Sadie was thoughtful for a moment. "Let me ask you something. What was the driving factor behind your coming west?"

Julia didn't even have to contemplate her answer. "To escape the life I was living in Boston."

"So is it fair to say that doing mission work wasn't truly your heart's desire, but just a solution that would be something your parents would approve of?"

"That sounds awful doesn't it?"

116

"No, it doesn't sound awful. I believe you really did think you could help people, and wanted to, but it wasn't a passion, and now that your plans have kind of derailed, you're rethinking some things."

"How do you do that?"

"Do what?"

"Read people like that and figure out what they're thinking?"

Sadie laughed. "That's my passion."

Julia raised an eyebrow at her and gave her a look that communicated she thought Sadie was pulling her leg.

"It's just a God-given gift. I like to help people by helping them figure out what's going on in their head."

"Well it's astounding. I've never met anyone like you."

"I hope that's a compliment."

"It is. I can talk to you, and you really understand where I'm coming from. Not a lot of people truly get a person, and you do. It's a complete gift. I really enjoy being here. You make me feel so welcome. You and your husband are both so warm and friendly. I greatly appreciate all your hospitality. I don't know what we would have done last night if we hadn't have found you. Things could have been so much worse."

"You see? You started being thankful, and already you have a better outlook on things."

"You're right." Julia sighed. "Now I just have to talk to Cash."

"I think it will be easier than you think it will."

"How so?"

"I don't think he has any plans to ship you out of here any time soon."

"Oh, I don't know. After the way I disregarded his advice yesterday, I'm pretty sure he wants nothing more than to see me return home."

"You just go talk to him, and be nice. I think everything will be fine."

"I hope so."

Julia stood up and walked down the steps of the porch toward the area where Cash was working. Sadie smiled to herself, noting that Julia hadn't picked up on her hint that Cash wouldn't want her to leave. That boy had feelings for her, Sadie was sure of it, and she couldn't wait to see how things would play out.

Chapter 21

Cash had noticed Julia sitting on the porch for quite some time, and truly hoped that she would come talk to him. He was finished with the work on the chicken coop, and wasn't sure if he should just pretend to still be working, or head up to the house. He didn't want to interrupt the conversation she was having with Sadie. He took off his hat and ran his fingers through his hair. Oh this was ridiculous. He would just go talk to her. He put his hat back on his head, and bent to pick up the tools he had been using. When he straightened up and turned around, he noticed she was walking toward him. His first impulse was to feign working on the coop again. Why did she have him so flustered?

She made her way to him and he took a deep breath in an attempt to calm the butterflies he felt simply because she was near.

"Hello Cash. I hope I'm not interrupting."

"No not at all. I just finished."

"Oh good."

She seemed to hesitate, and there was a moment of awkward pause between them, then they both began speaking at the same time, which caused them to both stop and nervously laugh.

Julia began again. "I don't mean to bother you, but I was wondering if it would be possible for you to take me into Estes Park. I need to replace my belongings, and I'll need to wire my parents and, tell them, something about what's going on here, although I'm not sure what."

Instantly Cash felt compassion on her and realized she indeed had nothing but the clothes on her back. He and Ben had nothing either, except that Cash kept his money roll in his boot.

He wasn't about to place it anywhere other than on his person while he was in that camp.

"Of course I can take you." He paused, then continued. "I'm so sorry about all your things. If I thought there was any way to salvage them, I would, but if I step foot back in that camp, well let's just say it wouldn't be pretty."

Julia considered this for a moment. "Does this mean you won't be working there anymore? Did I lose you your job too?"

"I was going to be moving on in a few days anyway. It really isn't a problem."

Julia was amazed that he honestly didn't seem the least bit upset. Either that or he was really good at hiding it. "I am so sorry Cash. This whole thing, it's all my fault. I didn't listen to you, and now you have no job, I didn't listen to Ben, and now he's lying in a bed, injured, and in pain. This isn't at all how I thought things would turn out."

Cash wanted to stay on her good side, but he was also curious what her plans were now, especially since she had no supplies. He supposed she could still drive around and visit folks, but he sensed a change in her demeanor, and wondered exactly what she did plan to do.

"Have you thought about what your next step will be?" He hoped the question wouldn't upset her.

"I'm not going home if that's what you mean, and I won't be accompanying Ben back to Lyons.

I don't really know what the answer is yet, but these mountains do something to me that I can't fully explain. I want to experience them in a very real and personal way."

Cash wasn't exactly sure how to take that. He was a little concerned that the stress and trauma she had endured the night before had gotten to her, and maybe she wasn't entirely thinking straight. "Well anything I can do to help you, I'd be happy to do."

"Thank you Cash, I appreciate that."

With that she turned around and headed back toward the house. Cash was astonished that she actually still had a desire to stay. He honestly figured she would be on the next train headed east as quickly as possible. There was something about her that he found so intriguing, and her independent spirit was entirely a big part of it. Where she would go from here, he had no idea, but he most definitely wanted to be there to guide her along the way.

Chapter 22

After lunch, Cash and Julia set out in the wagon for the town of Estes Park. Sadie had repaired the one dress Julia now owned, so she at least had something that actually fit her to wear in to town.

Julia seemed indifferent to the recent events, and appeared to be simply enjoying the scenery. Cash longed to reach out to her, and talk to her about all her deepest feelings. Here was a beautiful woman who had completely captured his attention, and he wanted to get to know her. He wanted to find out what made her tick, and what had really brought her out here in the first place. She kept quiet though, and other than an occasional comment about the terrain they were traveling through, she didn't say anything.

Cash didn't want to let this opportunity go, so he began talking to her about how he grew up, and all about his family's mining business. This seemed to interest her, so he shared all about how he had left home to seek his own fortune, rather than have it handed to him.

"What was it exactly that made you decide to leave? I mean your family and everything you left behind sounds idyllic."

"Oh it's definitely wonderful, but somehow I just had to figure things out on my own. Have you ever felt like all of your decisions have already been made for you? I mean surely being from Boston, your family had some expectations for you."

"Oh they definitely do. More times than I care to think about."

"Well, it's the same with me. I wanted to strike out on my own, make my own name for myself, make my own money."

"Why did you choose mining?"

"It was the logical choice since I'd grown up around it."

"But do you really enjoy it? Is it your passion?" Julia thought as she asked this question that she had no idea what her passion truly was and she wondered if Cash did.

"I wouldn't say it's my passion, no. I know a lot about it, it comes easily to me, and I guess when it came down to it I just picked something that I already knew how to do. I think I was more passionate about just being out on my own, and making my own way in the world. What about you? What's your passion?"

Julia dreaded the question, and wondered if she should just give him an answer that sounded good, but wasn't necessarily how she felt. No, she wanted to start living life the way that she wanted to, not how someone else might want her or expect her to. "That's what I'm trying to discover."

"Really? I figured you'd say to reach the lost, or minister to others."

"Why? Because I came out here to do missionary work?"

"Well, yes. I would think you'd have to be passionate about that to want to do it."

Julia exhaled loudly and suddenly felt very uncomfortable with the conversation. "Can we change the subject? I don't really feel like talking about this."

"Sure. What do you want to talk about?"

"Let's talk about you some more. Were your parents upset when you left home?"

"No I wouldn't say they were upset. Disappointed maybe, but I also know that they understood that I needed to get out from under their wing and do my own thing for awhile."

As much as Julia wanted to keep the conversation steered away from her, nearly everything Cash said was something she could relate to or something that she wished her parents had done. "My parents don't seem to understand that. I know a lot of it has to do with the fact that I'm not a man. Men are allowed, and almost expected to go out and do their own thing, but if a woman does it, it's preposterous."

Cash hesitated to ask Julia another question for fear she would shut him down again, so he decided to just try and be agreeable. "I think it's very brave that you came out here on your own, and that you were following your dream." Julia didn't respond, but did seem to be mulling over what Cash had just said. He wasn't sure what was bothering her, so he tried a different approach.

"What did you think of the mountains when you first saw them?"

Julia seemed to brighten at that. "Oh I loved them. That moment when Ben and I were driving in the wagon and they first came into view was a scene I will never forget. There's something so amazing about them that seems to draw me in and speak to me. I want to discover exactly what it is."

"You seem different somehow."

"What do you mean?"

"Well yesterday you seemed so focused and driven on what it was you wanted to accomplish, and today you seem to just be thinking things through."

"I guess I am. Last night was quite a blow to my confidence, and it really got me to thinking about exactly what it is I want to do out here. In all honesty Cash, I didn't leave home to be a missionary, I left home to leave home, and being a missionary was an acceptable way for me to do that with my parent's approval. I feel like a giant fake as a result, and am mortified of what you must think of me. I truly would be interested in helping people, I really would, It's just that now, I don't know, I think it will be difficult for me to want to put myself out there again."

"I don't think any less of you Julia. What you're saying is completely understandable. You went through a severe trauma last night, and I think it's normal to be a little unsure of what your next step should be. One thing I know for sure though, is whatever you choose to do, you will be great at it."

Again Julia didn't respond, and Cash knew it would take her some time to not feel badly about everything that had happened.

The town of Estes Park came into view and Julia's attention seemed to become focused on it. Cash wasn't sure, but he thought she looked a little uncomfortable.

"Are you alright?"

125

"Oh, I'll be fine. I guess I'm just thinking about when I first arrived in Lyons, and everything that has happened since then. Let's just say my confidence is at an all-time low, and I'm pretty unsure of things right now."

"It will be okay. We're just here to buy a few things, and then we can be on our way. Stick close to me and you'll be fine."

Cash parked the wagon outside of a general store and quickly hopped out in order to help Julia down. There were quite a few people milling about, and Julia was relieved that they all seemed to be caught up in their own affairs. She and Cash walked into the general store, and began looking around.

The selection was more than Julia had anticipated. The store was probably twice the size of the Coleman's back in Lyons, and Julia quickly relaxed and began selecting new clothing items that she would need.

She happened upon a small group of individuals talking with each other in a corner of the store. An item that she was looking at was close enough to them that she could overhear what they were saying. She soon found their conversation so interesting that she began listening to their every word.

"That's why people want to climb Longs Peak. I'm telling you, it will be the most fascinating adventure of your life. Now let's go over the equipment lists again to make sure everyone has what they need."

Julia realized she was staring at the young man who had been leading the conversation. He happened to look up and see her looking at him so he smiled and spoke to her.

"Can I help you miss?"

"Are you going to climb a mountain?"

"I do climb mountains. I climb them every chance I get. I'm leading an expedition up Longs in a few days. Have you ever climbed a mountain?"

"No, but I am fascinated by them."

"They are fascinating that's for sure. There's nothing like standing on the top of one. It's almost like you're standing on top of the world. Longs Peak is the tallest mountain around here. It's over 14,000 feet high."

"That sounds amazing."

"Have you ever thought about climbing a mountain?"

"I don't really know. I'm pretty new to the area, and I don't know much about them yet, but I definitely want to learn."

"You're more than welcome to come with us if you like."

"Really?"

At this point, Cash who had caught the last few pieces of the conversation wandered over and introduced himself. "I think mountain climbing might be a little out of her league at the moment, she's a complete greenhorn when it comes to the outdoors."

"Well, that doesn't mean she can't learn."

"That's right Cash." Julia replied with a touch of irritation to her voice. "It doesn't mean I can't learn."

"I think we need to finish shopping and head back." Cash smiled, then guided Julia away from the mountaineer. "Thanks for your time, I appreciate it."

"If you ever change your mind, I'm always around. Name's Mills, Enos Mills."

Cash shook his hand then turned and anticipated helping Julia with the rest of her purchases, but she was nowhere to be seen. He looked all over the store, but couldn't find her. Finally he went outside and found her sitting on a bench along the boardwalk.

"Where'd you go?" He asked in a friendly manner.

"Don't ever do that again."

"Do what?" Cash was honestly confused by her response.

"Speak for me. If I want to talk with someone, I'm going to talk to them, and I don't need you coming over and acting like I'm a piece of property."

Cash was caught completely off guard and wasn't sure what to say. "Are you talking about those mountaineers?"

"Yes, I'm talking about the mountaineers. I was very fascinated by what they had to say, and I don't appreciate you barging in and ending my conversation."

Cash was speechless, and looked at her with regret. "I'm sorry, I just didn't think you knew what you were getting yourself into. If you want to talk with them go right ahead." He waved his hand toward the store where they most likely still were.

Julia sat still for a moment, then got up abruptly. "Thank you, I believe I will." With that she flounced down the boardwalk and back into the store.

Cash sat on the bench trying to process what had just happened. He honestly didn't mean to upset her. He was only trying to help her, since she had mentioned feeling uncomfortable and unsure of herself upon arriving in town.

He stood and made his way back into the store to complete his purchases, then waited for Julia in the wagon. She came along several minutes later, carrying several parcels and seeming quite pleased with herself. She avoided eye contact with him and settled herself in the back of the wagon instead of sitting on the seat next to him.

It was a long, quiet, tension-filled drive back to the Cumming's homestead. Cash didn't want her to be angry with him, but he honestly didn't feel that he had done anything wrong. He was just looking out for her. Longs Peak was a dangerous undertaking, and he knew she had no idea what all it would involve.

That evening at dinner, Julia made an announcement. "I'm going to climb Longs Peak."

Cash dropped his fork out of shock, but said nothing. Sadie and Carl looked at each other, as if trying to decide who should speak first. Carl took the reins.

"Longs Peak you say? How did that come about?"

"I met a mountaineer in town today who is leading an expedition in a few days. We got to talking, and he convinced me what a thrilling experience it would be, so I'm going to do it."

"What's his name?" Sadie asked as she got up to pour everyone another round of coffee, since she had a feeling this conversation might last for awhile.

"Enos Mills." Cash answered for her.

Julia shot Cash a disgusted look then spoke up. "Yes, Enos Mills. Apparently he's led quite a few people up there. It's his passion."

"Oh yes, we know him." Carl took a sip of his coffee. "He has a homestead not far from here."

Cash, Sadie, and Carl all kind of looked at each other to see who would be the one to truly delve into this conversation.

Sadie smiled at Julia. "So what made you decide to climb Longs Peak?"

"I don't know really. I was feeling so down and discouraged about how things turned out in the mining camp, and when I overheard Enos talking in town with the others who are going on the expedition, it sounded so exciting, that I decided I wanted to be a part of it."

"Of course he's going to make it sound exciting, he's trying to drum up business." Cash grumbled into his coffee cup.

"So, umm, have you done much research on the climb?" Sadie tried to keep the conversation rolling because ever since Cash and Julia had come back from town she could tell something was going on. They hadn't spoken a word to each other since they returned. Now she knew why.

Cash snickered, downed the last of his coffee, and got up abruptly. "If you'll excuse me, I think I need to get some air."

Julia ignored him completely and proceeded to answer Sadie's question. "No, but there are other people going, and Enos is a qualified guide. I thought I would just let him take the lead in telling me what to do."

Carl cleared his throat. "Julia, I hate to burst your bubble, but Longs Peak is a dangerous mountain. People have died up there. It's not just a friendly nature walk, it's a serious mountaineering endeavor, and I don't think you know enough about what all will be required of you to safely make the trip."

Julia seemed to completely deflate. "I understand that it will be difficult, but I thought that it would be a good experience for me. I like to try new things."

Sadie smiled gently at her. "It would be a good experience, but we just want to make sure that you fully study up on it and completely understand what all will be involved before you actually go do it. This isn't the kind of thing you should make a hasty decision about. Learn all you can about the climb, and then decide if it is indeed something you really want to do, and is something you are passionate about."

There was that word again. Passion. Why did it seem like everyone understood their own passion for things, but Julia had such a hard time finding hers.

"I, I don't know what to say. I think I need to be alone for awhile. Excuse me." Julia got up from the table and went to the front door. She thought she would take a walk around the property. The sun had just set, but there was still enough light left to see where she was going. Once she shut the door behind her, she quickly made her way down the steps and was honestly thinking about running at full speed for a couple of minutes to burn off her frustration when she heard a voice behind her in the shadows of the porch.

"Do you even know which one of those mountains is Longs Peak?"

Julia whirled around to see Cash move from the porch where he had been and make his way down the steps to stand right in front of her.

"Well, do you?"

Julia tried to retain her confident attitude, but she knew Cash had her on this point. "What does it matter? I don't have to take a geography test before I go. I'll have a guide."

"Just another reason why you shouldn't go. You'll have a guide Julia, a guide. He won't actually do the hiking for you. You have no idea what you're getting yourself into. Longs Peak is that mountain right there!" Cash pointed forcefully to the massive mountain in the distance. "Right there, right in the middle, the tallest one around. What are you going to do when you're way up there above treeline and maybe the weather starts changing, and suddenly it's windy or raining and the rocks get slick, or maybe the clouds move in and engulf you and you can't see two feet in front of your face. What are you going to do then Julia? Have you studied the route? Do you understand exactly where you're going, or where you need to head next?"

"Alright!" Julia put her hand up to stop him. "I get it Cash. I'm sorry I'm not as perfect as you. I'm sorry I don't have everything figured out as perfectly as you do. Although I have to say you've got to have some issues yourself otherwise you wouldn't have run away from home. Were your father's expectations too high for you, and you thought if you struck out on

133

your own you wouldn't have to continually impress him?"

"Are you really going to talk about running away from home? Because I think that's your area of expertise. The only difference is I didn't have to lie to my parents to get their stamp of approval on what I was doing."

"I didn't lie!"

"Oh, well not to them maybe, but you definitely lied to yourself. You don't know what you want. One minute you insist on being a missionary to a bunch of miners who have absolutely no intention of listening to you, the next you want to run off and climb a mountain that you know absolutely nothing about. What do you want Julia? What are doing out here? Why did you travel 2000 miles by yourself? What is it that you're running away from, or what is it that you're looking for?"

"I want "

"What? What it is it? What do you want?"

Julia tried to talk again. "I want…" She shook her head, unable to express her feelings.

"What? What do you want? Cat got your tongue?"

Julia's eyes flashed with frustration. "I want to learn how to live!"

Cash hesitated. What did she mean by that?

Julia sighed. "My whole life I was always expected to be a certain way."

134

Cash could relate to that. Part of what Julia had said was true. His parents did have high expectations, and maybe subconsciously that had influenced his decision to strike out on his own, but it definitely wasn't the main reason, and he definitely didn't run away.

She continued. "I thought coming west would free me from the confines I felt in Boston, and in some ways it has, but in other ways I find myself more confused than ever."

Cash didn't speak, but just looked at her.

She avoided eye contact with him and simply stared off into the distance without seeing what she was actually looking at as she continued. "I want to have an impact on this world, and I do want to help others, but I think most of all I want to discover who I really am. I've been told how I was supposed to be my whole life, but I knew that wasn't really me. I wasn't happy in Boston. I had to find a way out, and when I did, I thought it would be the answer to helping me discover who I should be in life." She looked down briefly before continuing. "But so far it hasn't."

Cash spoke in a more subdued tone than what he had been, but he still wanted to communicate his concern, and disdain for what she was doing. "And you think running off and climbing a mountain you know nothing about will help you discover that?"

"I don't know. I don't seem to know anything anymore. I just thought it seemed like a once in a lifetime opportunity."

Cash sighed deeply. He wanted to groan with frustration, because of the conflicting feelings he had towards her. She made him feel things he had never felt before. Just the sight of her both excited him, and made him want to argue with her at the same time. Finally he replied. "If you really want to climb mountains, it's definitely exciting, and can be a soul-searching adventure, but don't start with Longs. Let me lead you up some mountains. We can start with ones that aren't nearly as dangerous."

Julia looked into his eyes for the first time in several minutes. "You'd do that for me?"

Cash shrugged. "Why not? I think I have experience in rescuing you from dangerous situations, so I think it would be only fitting that I be the one to introduce you to these mountains."

"What about your job? What are your plans for that?"

"Tell you what. There are plenty of mountains we can climb between here and Lulu City, where I was planning on heading next. Why don't you come with me, and see if maybe there's someplace you can fit in there."

Julia thought about that for a moment. "It's a mining town?"

"Yes, a legitimate town with families, and stores, and even a church. It's isolated deep in the mountains though, so maybe you'll find people more in need, and you can give your missionary work another shot."

Julia seemed to brighten at that thought. "I don't have any supplies, but maybe I can get some in Estes before we head out."

Cash was thoughtful for a moment. "If you're really serious about this, the best way to see the mountains is to go deep into them. We can go on horseback, and then when we come to a mountain you want to climb, we can tie the horses up, summit the mountain, then come back for them. We should only take the bare necessities. Maybe you try just offering people a smile and a kind word, then helping them out with chores they need done, and not worry so much about having something to give them."

Julia thought that over. "I suppose you're right. If I have to buy a horse, I definitely wouldn't have money left for anything else."

Cash pressed her just a bit to see how serious she was about this. "Are you sure this is what you want to do? It won't be easy."

"I want to find myself Cash. I want to discover who I really am, and I think the best way to do that is to spend time in these mountains. I feel a connection to them that I don't fully understand, but it's like they're calling me, and I know that I have to answer. I have to go and see where they lead me."

Cash felt an excitement within him at the thought of being alone with Julia for days on end. He would really get to know her, which was what he wanted. He also knew he was in for an incredible undertaking. Julia could be stubborn, and by the time they got to Lulu City, he may be ready to toss her off the nearest cliff. He knew one thing for sure though, it was a chance he was willing to take.

Chapter 23

Ben sat propped up comfortably with pillows on the porch of the Cumming's homestead, sipping tea and listening to Cash and Julia talk over their plans. He was feeling stronger every day, and planned to make the journey home to Lyons by the end of the week.

Julia had been in contact with her parents, and let them know she would be heading over the Continental Divide to the town of Lulu City. The news didn't thrill them, but there really wasn't much they could say with her being 2000 miles away. Her father had wired her more money when she had told them she would be purchasing a horse.

She had let them know that she had purchased a great deal of supplies when she had first arrived, so they assumed she had distributed them to needy families. She didn't correct them even though she felt terrible not telling them the whole story of what had taken place, but she also knew they would be incredibly upset if they knew the truth, and she actually thought of withholding the information from them as a way of sparing them from something that would cause them great distress.

She and Cash had purchased the things they needed, and keeping everything to a bare minimum, they had only what was absolutely necessary to get them across the mountains. They were now discussing how soon they would be leaving.

Cash wanted to get going as soon as possible, since the weeks of summer were definitely numbered in the Rockies, and he wanted to ensure that they were over the divide before the snows began in a few short weeks. Julia didn't want to leave Ben until he was fully healed and ready to return to Lyons.

"You best do what Cash suggests. He's right about the weather, and there's nothing you can do for me. I'm feeling better every day."

"I know Ben, but I still feel like it's my fault that you're in this condition to begin with, and I would feel awful if we just up and left while you were still trying to recover."

"That's nonsense Julia. We've been over this a dozen times. All has been forgiven, and it's time to look toward the future. I knew that you would find your way up onto these mountains one of these days. I could just tell by the way you looked at them with such fascination. I'm glad you have a good man like Cash to lead you up there. I'll be thinking about you two every day when I'm back home."

"Alright Ben, I'll go, but just know that I will be forever grateful for all that you've done for me, and if you ever need anything, I will be there for you. I would do anything for you Ben, I hope you know that."

"I do Miss Julia. You've got a bright future ahead of you, and I look forward to hearing about all that you'll accomplish. I've enjoyed the time we've spent together, and I wish you all the best."

Sadie came out on the porch in the middle of the conversation. "Alright you two, you make it sound like you're leaving this minute. I need some folks to eat this big dinner I'm making. Who's hungry?"

Julia wiped a tear that had formed as Ben was speaking those kind words to her. "Oh Sadie, you're such a marvelous cook, and you've absolutely spoiled us rotten since we've been here. Whatever will we do without you?"

"Oh you'll be just fine. You folks needed some looking after for a few days, but you're good to go now. Time to move on to the next set of adventures."

"I like the sound of that. Life *can* be an adventure can't it?"

"Life can be anything you want it to be." Sadie swatted at a fly with the dish towel she was carrying. "Now come in here and eat."

Everyone laughed and Cash helped Ben stand, then move slowly into the cabin. Julia picked up the pillows he'd been using. She thought over Sadie's words. Life truly could be anything she wanted it to be. Things hadn't exactly worked out the way she had thought they would, but maybe that was simply part of discovering who she was, and who she was meant to be. There might be bumps in the road, but Julia was determined to make the time she had in the mountains an adventure, and reveal exactly who she was, and where she was going in life. That would be the greatest adventure she could imagine.

Chapter 24

Two days later, Cash and Julia set out on horseback, stocked with everything they would need to make it for at least a week in the mountains. They would take their time, and when they came to a mountain that looked like a pleasant destination, they would stop and climb it. Julia was excited. She was fully rested, and felt as though she had worked through the difficulties she had encountered thus far.

She would be forever grateful for the kindness and generosity offered to herself, Cash and Ben by Sadie and Dr. Carl Cummings. She and Cash had both tried to offer them money, which they had repeatedly turned down, so they had both left some on the nightstands of their rooms.

Ben was healing nicely, and would soon make the trip back to Lyons. Julia promised to get in touch with him as soon as she possibly could, to both check on him, and to let him know how she and Cash were doing as well.

The morning was dawning clear and cool, as they rode along, making their way northwest to begin their trek into the mountains. Cash wasn't completely familiar with the area they would be traveling through, but he had been learning all he could about it while they were at the Cummings, and Ben had given him several pointers, since he had actually climbed several mountains in the area. Cash had also bought a map one of the times they were in Estes Park, and had been studying it extensively.

Julia had studied the map with him as well, and was fascinated by the ground they would be covering. Their first stop that they had both agreed would be a good place to start, would be Estes Cone. It was a pointy little mountain that Julia had gazed upon several times from the Cummings homestead. It was quite close by, and Cash said they should be able to be on the summit by noon.

Julia took the time to take in the beautiful surroundings as they rode their horses through the cool woods. The air was so fresh and clean, and she felt content as she rode through it, feeling as though she had turned a page in her life, and was beginning a new chapter.

She had a sort of nervous excitement coursing through her the further they went. Soon Cash would say they were at a place where they would tie the horses, and set off on foot. She was actually going to climb a mountain. Never in all her life when she was living in Boston, did she ever imagine that she would someday be out hiking in the Colorado Rockies.

She put all the negative thoughts behind her that she had only used the guise of being a missionary to get her away from her life in Boston. She completely had intentions of doing just that when she first came out here, but things had changed, and she realized that she honestly needed to devote some time to simply finding out exactly who she was. She couldn't very effectively help others if she didn't even know the answers to her own life.

"This is it."

Julia was brought out of her barrage of thoughts, back to the moment and realized it was time to start hiking. "We're here?"

"Yep, we'll go on foot from here. Are you ready?"

Julia smiled broadly as she replied. "Absolutely. I couldn't be more excited."

Cash had to smile back and enjoy how relaxed and happy Julia had seemed the past few days ever since she had finally opened up and revealed her true feelings and desires about leaving home and being in the mountains. He didn't blame her. She had pure motives, and she was just trying to figure out her life, kind of like he was. They had quite a bit in common actually, both striking out on their own to discover who they really were. When Julia had asked him if mining was his passion, it definitely struck a chord in him. He knew that it wasn't, and he had answered her that he was passionate about being out on his own and figuring things out. He guessed that's what he was passionate about. Was that even was a thing *to* be passionate about? Figuring out your life? He would have to talk to Julia more about it. He had a feeling they could probably both benefit from each other's life stories.

They made their way up the trail which was rather difficult to follow. The woods were thick and they obstructed any views they might have on the way up of the surrounding mountains. They paused occasionally to catch their breath, and discuss how much further they thought it might be. Julia was doing remarkably well and Cash was proud of her. She really seemed to be enjoying herself, and he was encouraged by seeing her seem this comfortable in the wilderness. She might become a great mountaineering woman yet.

A while later they topped out at the base of some cliffs, and Cash knew they were near the rocky top of the mountain that had been so visible from the Cummings homestead.

"Okay Julia, are you ready for this? We get to do some climbing."

Julia looked with uncertainty at the towering mounds of rock looming overhead but appeared undaunted. "Just tell me what to do, and I'll do it." She replied with a smile on her face.

Cash went first and had Julia right behind. He pointed out where she should grab onto a rock, and where she should step, and praised her as she moved with amazing ease. Soon they reached the top.

"Is that it?" Julia looked around to see if they would have to climb further.

"No, that's it. We're here."

"That was fun. I could do that all day."

The summit was interesting looking, dotted with gnarled dwarfed trees, attempting to grow at the high altitude where it was nearly impossible for them to do so. It wasn't a nice even rounded "top" like Julia thought it might be. It was kind of spread out, at different levels, and Cash and Julia visited each one, clambering over the boulders, and seeing all that there was to see.

"Your first mountain. What do you think?"

"I love it! That was the most exciting thing I've ever done. Look at the views! Look at that mountain there. It's so big. What is it?"

"That's Longs Peak."

"What? *That's* Longs? Oh my. It's so rugged looking." Julia looked down for a moment then turned to look at Cash full on. "You were right to stop me from climbing it. I would have been in way over my head. It's much more fun taking it

145

slow. I really appreciate all you're doing for me Cash. I don't deserve your kindness."

"Oh don't be silly. I don't know that any of us deserve anything. We all make mistakes from time to time, we're only human. It's what we learn from our mistakes that matters."

"That's true. Well, I just want you to know that I'm so grateful for what you're doing for me. I think I did pretty well on this mountain. What do you think?"

Cash laughed. "Yes Julia, you climbed it like you climb them all the time. I think you're ready to move on to the bigger ones."

"Bigger? Not Longs though, right?"

"No, not Longs. Cash pointed slightly to the northwest. See those mountains over there? That's where we're headed next. Those two right there are Flattop Mountain, and Hallett Peak."

"Oh my. They are big. Are you sure they aren't as rugged as Longs?"

"No, you'll do fine. Ben gave me plenty of pointers and information. I think you'll love them." Cash smiled at Julia and she smiled back. He had to admit he felt flutters of attraction for her, and he wondered if she felt any. He watched her as she made her way around the summit, taking it all in, and he knew that he wanted to protect her, and take care of her, and teach her about the mountains, and just be with her. He realized at that moment that he was falling for her, and it scared him a little, but only because he wasn't sure that she would feel the same way towards him. One thing was for sure though, he would treasure this time that they had together, because there was something about Julia that he never wanted to let go of.

Chapter 25

Cash and Julia made their way down Estes Cone, and back to their horses, where they continued on. Their stop for the night would be Bear Lake, which Cash explained would be right in the shadow of the two mountains he had pointed out to her earlier. When they would stop for breaks, Julia would pull out the map and attempt to match up the mountains and landmarks she was seeing, with what she saw on the map. She found it fascinating, and wanted to learn all she could about the area they were passing through. Cash enjoyed watching her, and had to admit she seemed like a completely different person than when he first met her. She was so much more relaxed, and interested in discovering things, rather than intense and trying to make things happen.

They arrived at Bear Lake late that afternoon, and while the lake was truly beautiful, Julia's attention was drawn to the mountains that towered over it. "We're really headed up there tomorrow?"

"Yep, are you nervous?"

"I'd be lying if I said no. I feel like they look so much bigger than what we did today."

"They are, but that doesn't mean you can't do it. It just means the payoff will be all the more spectacular."

"That's a wonderful way of thinking about it. I won't be scared with you by my side."

Cash felt the flutters again, but tried to brush them aside. They sat next to the fire Cash had built, and he was glad the evening was so peaceful. There wasn't a breath of wind, and the lake was as still as a sheet of glass. "Julia, remember when you asked me if mining was my passion?"

Julia looked up from gazing at the fire, and pulled the blanket she had wrapped around her a little tighter. "Yes. That was the day that we, well, let's just say we got a few things out in the open."

Cash smiled. "Yes, exactly. That question really sparked something in me though. Mining definitely isn't my passion, and in all honesty I'm not really sure what my passion is in life. I do know that I want to discover it though."

"You don't know how good it makes me feel to hear you say that." Julia was astonished at his revelation. "Ever since the incident at the mining camp, I've felt like I'm the lost one, wandering around with no direction. Not to say that you feel the same way I do, but it's just nice to know I'm not the only one struggling to figure my life out."

"You were also right about my parent's expectations being high."

148

Julia blushed at the memory and shook her head.

Cash continued. "No, you were right. I mean from what you've said I don't think they influenced my decisions in the same way yours did, but it was definitely a motivating factor in my decision to strike out on my own."

Julia put a smug smile on her face. "Hmmm, could it be Cash Parker, that you and I are actually quite similar?"

Cash laughed and smiled back. "I think it's definitely a possibility."

"How many siblings do you have?"

"I have two older sisters."

Julia's eyes grew wide. "So do I." She thought for a moment then asked him another question. "What was your favorite thing to eat that Sadie cooked for us while we were there?"

Cash was enjoying this game. "Well it was all fantastic, but my absolute favorite was her biscuits and gravy."

"Yes!" Julia exclaimed. That was the best thing I think I've ever eaten.

They both laughed together and then Cash took a turn at asking the question. "What's your favorite thing to do in the mountains?"

Julia knew her answer immediately, but wasn't sure if it was an exciting enough activity.

Cash sensed her hesitation. "Well, what is it?"

"I hope you don't think it's silly, but ever since my first night spent outside in the mountains, I've been captivated by how beautiful and bright the stars are. I just love being able to lay under them and look at them." She shrugged after giving her answer.

Cash paused a beat then answered. "It's funny that you say that, because that is exactly the answer I would give. I have long enjoyed the night sky. It's kind of like an old friend who is always there night after night, and it's comforting, especially since I left home."

Julia was in awe at his response. "That's beautiful Cash. I'm so glad you feel that way. The first time I saw the stars, I knew that looking at them from then on would always be special to me."

They both sat quietly for a moment, then Julia spoke. "Do you want to look at them now?"

Cash looked at her, her face illuminated by the fire, her long hair cascading down over her shoulders, and her woolen trail blanket wrapped around her. She had such a sweet innocence about her, and he loved how the experience of the mountains was all so fresh and new to her.

"Of course." He grabbed his trail blanket and spread it out on the ground, then sat down and patted the spot next to him.

He laid back and Julia joined him, sitting down next to him while she unwrapped her blanket from around herself. "We can share." She said as she shook it to open it up fully.

She began to lie down and impulsively Cash held his arm out to the side and said gently. "Come here."

Julia willingly snuggled up against him, her face against his chest, his arm wrapped around her. They spread the blanket over them, and Julia exhaled happily as she snuggled in even closer to him. "This is nice."

"Yes it is." Cash was glad there was no hesitation on her part. He relished the feel of her lying next to him, and knew that he would be perfectly content to stay there forever.

"So we're at over 9000 feet in elevation now, right?"

Cash smiled at how her mind was always working. "That's right."

"Look how close the stars look here. Can you imagine what they would look like on top of the divide?"

"It would be pretty amazing."

"Can we gaze at the stars on top of the divide?"

"I suppose we could, but it might be really cold and windy."

"Well I wasn't saying we'd spend the night up there, but just for a little bit. We'll be up above the trees right?"

"That's right."

"Can you imagine how beautiful that will be? Nothing around to obstruct our vision. Just the huge night sky spread over us like a canopy. Let's do it Cash. Please?"

Cash had to laugh at how she found such joy in the things around them. "I can't promise you it won't be just horribly cold or that the wind won't be brutal."

"I'll take that chance. I just have to see them. Don't you want to see them Cash?"

He smiled. "Alright, you talked me into it. We'll make our camp on the other side of the divide tomorrow afternoon, then head back up to the top in the evening so we can look at the stars."

"Oh that sounds wonderful. Doesn't that sound wonderful to you?"

"Absolutely." He gave her a squeeze with the arm he held her with, and thought how at this exact moment, he had never been happier in all his life than he was right now.

Chapter 26

The first streaks of pink shot across the sky, and Cash roused himself to stoke the fire. Even though it was August, at this altitude it still got unpleasantly cold during the night. He glanced over at Julia who still slept peacefully. Last night with her had been wonderful. He never dreamed he could feel this way about another person, and what made it special was the fact that he felt they were both not only discovering things about each other, but learning about themselves as well. Being alone in the mountains was always

152

therapeutic, but experiencing it with someone like Julia took things to an entirely different level.

By the time Julia stirred, Cash had a roaring fire going, which made the campsite pleasantly warm. They took their time getting ready, sharing more stories with each other over their morning coffee. By the time they struck camp and headed off, the sun had risen enough to begin to warm the chilly air.

They rode silently for the most part in the early hours of the morning, simply enjoying the scenery, and making an occasional comment about an unusual rock or a pretty tree that they passed. The mornings seemed almost sacred in the mountains. The horse's hooves breaking the stillness that surrounded them seemed to be the only noise that should be allowed.

After a while they came to an overlook, and dismounted their horses to have a look around. Cash consulted the map, and Julia edged in right next to him so she could see as well.

"That must be Dream Lake down there." Julia pointed over the edge of the overlook to a long narrow lake below them. "And look at how close Hallett Peak is."

Cash had to smile. "You're learning quickly. Soon you'll know the mountains better than I do."

Julia shot him a smirky smile. "Maybe I will. Wouldn't you be surprised if I actually did?"

"Not at all. You're an intelligent woman Julia. You can do anything you set your mind to."

Julia was genuinely appreciative. "Thank you Cash. That means a lot to me."

They continued on, and soon rose above treeline, which was Julia's first experience with that. She was completely astounded, looking in every direction, and admiring every view that she saw.

"This is so wonderful Cash! I never knew what things would look like from up here. I was in awe when I first saw the mountains from down below, but I never dreamed that I would ever see the view from the top, let alone actually be standing on top of them."

"It is something special. It never gets old."

"How many mountains have you climbed?"

"Oh, quite a few. There are mountains at home that we climbed over and over, but every chance I got when I would go someplace new, I'd check out the mountains. This is the first time I've climbed anything around here though. I didn't have a chance to do anything big while I was working at Eugenia, just hiking in the woods right around the mine. In fact that's what I was heading off to do when you and Ben arrived at the camp."

Cash hoped he wasn't bringing up an unpleasant memory for her. It was actually one that he cherished because it was the day that he met her.

She didn't seem to mind though, and simply seemed in awe of all that he'd been able to do thus far in his life. "You see, I hear you talk about all the time you've spent hiking, and I think it's really impressive." She gave him kind of an impish smile. "It really doesn't give people like me much of a chance in the life experiences department. No one ever wishes they spent more time living in a city. You have an unfair advantage living in the mountains. There's no way I can ever compete with that."

He shot her a playful suggestion. "Who says life has to be a competition?"

She laughed. "It doesn't, but I'd like you to think I'm as interesting as you are. Unfortunately concerts, balls, and tea parties don't even come close to what you have out here."

"What are you saying? I think a tea party would be fascinating."

"Oh stop!"

"No really. You'll have to show me Boston sometime."

She smiled in that coy little flirtatious way that he was beginning to find irresistible. "I'd much rather you show me even more of Colorado."

"That can definitely be arranged."

They continued on and soon came to another overlook. This time Julia pulled out the map to see what it was they were looking at. "Emerald Lake." She announced. "Oh it's beautiful, but it's so far down there. Look at that. It almost makes

155

me a little dizzy looking at that." She grabbed Cash's arm and laughed as she stepped back from the edge. "Have you ever felt so free? This is wonderful. I'm simply having the best time."

"I'm glad Julia. You deserve it."

Soon after the Emerald Lake overlook, the trail began heading pretty much due west, and it was obvious they were getting closer to their destination.

"This isn't bad at all. The horses can walk the whole way. We haven't encountered any climbing like we did yesterday on Estes Cone."

"It's a good trail. There had to be a way to access both sides of the divide, and this is definitely nice and smooth."

"Do you think that's the summit up there?" Julia pointed at the highest spot of land she could see, which was still quite a ways ahead of them, and off to their right."

"Maybe. Sometimes with mountains what you think is the top actually isn't. It's called a false summit, because when you get up to the point you were eyeballing, you see that it's not the summit at all, and the mountain keeps going."

"It's amazing how big they really are. They kind of just keep going and going when you're actually on them."

"Yep. They can definitely keep you guessing."

"Look at how different Hallett Peak looks from this angle. The part of it that you see from Bear

Lake isn't the summit at all. From here it looks like a rounded hump."

Cash smiled. She was almost like a kid in a candy store with all of her observations. It was like she was discovering all sorts of new flavors of candy that she didn't even know existed. "Oh yeah, look at that. That's interesting."

Soon after, the horses topped out on the area that Julia had spotted from down below, and it was expansive. It was obvious they were on top of the Continental Divide.

"Well what do you know, there wasn't a false summit. I was seeing the top after all."

"Good for you little miss smartypants."

Julia feigned shock at his comment, then laughed heartily. "I think I know why they call it Flattop Mountain. It's definitely flat up here. And big. Look at it, it seems to go on forever.

The wind was definitely stronger on the summit, but not unpleasantly so. It was a nice stiff breeze to combat the strong, high altitude rays of the sun.

Cash and Julia both felt hungry, so while they took a break, and were sitting there eating, Cash couldn't help but notice how much Julia was gazing at Hallett Peak, which was the next mountain over from Flattop. It was close, and Cash could tell by looking at it that it wouldn't be a difficult climb, but it would definitely be exciting for Julia. He took a look at the sky, and didn't see any storm clouds building. It was still early enough in the day, so he made the suggestion.

"Do you want to climb Hallett Peak?"

"Do I? You bet I do. It looks like fun."

"That it does. We can leave our things here, it won't take us long."

They set off after they finished eating with Cash leading the way. Julia was simply brimming with excitement and chattered the whole way.

"It seems like it's right there, but we keep walking and aren't to the base of it yet. Oh this is so exciting. Look at those other mountains over there. I'll have to get the map out when we get back and see what their names are."

Cash listened to her carry on and smiled. He found her enthusiasm endearing. Before long they reached the base of Hallett, and began climbing. It was basically like climbing a staircase of rock to get to the top. Definitely not as strenuous or as challenging as getting to the top of Estes Cone, but more exciting than Flattop. It felt like they were actually climbing a mountain.

Before long they reached the summit, and Julia was mesmerized. "Oh Cash! Look at this! This feels like a real summit of something. This is so exciting."

 The summit was fairly small, and definitely gave the feeling of being on top of the world. Julia looked around at all the other mountains, then noticed a big one in the distance, that definitely stood out apart from the others. "Look at Longs Peak from this side. It looks completely different than it did from the Cumming's homestead."

"Well look at you, able to identify Longs from its other side. Have you been studying the map when I wasn't looking?"

"Honestly I just took a guess. It's the tallest one around, so I figured it was Longs. But it does look different from here doesn't it?"

Cash laughed at her answer. "That was a good guess. I can see the allure of Longs. It is a fascinating mountain that definitely stands out."

Julia took a deep breath in and held her arms out wide. "I'm so happy to be here, and to be experiencing this. I've climbed two mountains already which is way more than I ever thought I would accomplish."

"Three. Don't forget Flattop."

"Oh, of course. It almost didn't seem like a summit, since it's so wide. We did ride the horses to the top of that one though, so I guess we cheated."

"We won't tell anyone."

Julia smiled. "So where do we go from here?"

"Well, see that trail heading over there toward the west?"

"Yes."

"That's the Tonohutu Trail, and we'll follow it along the divide for a while, then it eventually takes us down the other side. If you like, we can follow the trail for a ways, then skirt off of it, and make a camp at a lower elevation, then come back up on the divide tonight to watch the stars."

"That sounds perfect. I would really love that. Can we look at the map together to find a good place to break off from the trail and make camp?"

"Of course. If you don't already have it memorized."

"Maybe I do, and I have an ulterior motive, and I'm lulling you into a false sense of security."

"Uh oh, I'll have to watch out for you." Cash was enjoying this playful banter between the two of them. He never would have guessed Julia could ever be this laid back and relaxed when he first met her.

They descended Hallett, and made their way back over to where the horses were waiting. There were some building storm clouds in the distance, but they were still quite far off, and it was too soon to tell exactly what direction they were heading.

They consulted the map, and Julia thought that descending to Ptarmigan Lake looked like a good place to strike off trail and make camp.

"Works for me. We should probably head that way soon so we're not up on top if an afternoon storm hits."

They mounted their horses and headed off along the trail. Julia raised her head and put her nose into the wind, relishing every moment that they spent in this magnificent place. It was almost like being in another world. The tundra stretched on for miles, and the views were unparalleled to anything Julia had seen before. She wanted to soak in every aspect of what she was seeing into her senses. She wanted to feel this moment forever within her.

Every so often, Cash would stop and they would consult the map. When they reached the point where they should leave the trail, they turned and headed off along more of the indescribable tundra that was dotted with wildflowers here and there.

"Isn't it something how those little flowers can grow in such a harsh environment?"

"They're determined, and so they make it. Kind of like you."

"Oh that's so kind Cash. It's like you as well. We're both determined people. Determined to discover who we really are and what we're supposed to be doing with our lives."

The land began to slope downward, and soon Ptarmigan Lake came into view. The terrain then became quite steep, leading down to the lake, but the tundra continued all the way down, which made for a smooth descent. When they finally reached the lake, and Julia found the spot absolutely beautiful.

Cash looked around and noted how far they still were above treeline. "We'll definitely get wet if rain moves in. Since we have the horses and can make better time, we should probably head down even more into the woods, so that we have the protection of the trees."

Julia looked around as well and agreed, especially once she heard a rumble of thunder in the distance.

Cash led the way and called back to her. "We can wait out the storm in the woods, then we can come back up this evening."

They followed the outlet stream from the lake, and eventually made their way into a heavily wooded area, where they unloaded the horses to set up camp. Cash found a spot that was well sheltered with numerous tree limbs, which would provide adequate protection from any rain that might come.

They had just finished setting things up when the wind picked up and the sky unloaded on them. Julia sat on a soft bed of pine needles and watched Cash start a fire. Once he had it going sufficiently enough, he joined Julia and together they sat, enjoying the woodsy smells and the heat from the fire.

"I think I could get used to this."

"What? Sitting out in the rain?"

Julia laughed. "No, camping out. Living out in nature, being in the very depths of the wilderness. It's so healing."

"The company isn't bad either."

"No, the company isn't bad at all. In fact I like the company very much."

Her words hung in the air, and suddenly the only sound was the soft pattering of rain around them. Neither of them spoke and Cash ventured to look in her direction. She felt his eyes on her so she turned and looked at him as well. Cash had the impulse to kiss her, but second guessed himself, not being sure how she would react. He looked deep into her brown eyes, and knew that he was falling in love with her.

The moment between them seemed to last forever, and just when Cash thought he should get up and tend the fire, or check on the horses, or just do *something*, she leaned forward and kissed him, stopping him right in his tracks, and completely surprising him.

Her lips were so soft, and he responded immediately, kissing her back. At first he tried to sort out the barrage of thoughts running through his mind, ranging from disbelief that *she* would actually initiate a kiss, to just simple excitement that this was actually happening, but then he decided to simply quit thinking and focus on enjoying the moment.

The moment lasted for several moments, and when she finally pulled back and looked at him, he was in complete awe of the amazing woman in front of him.

She smiled as she spoke. "I realize that wasn't exactly the customary way that things like that

163

happen. I hope you don't mind, I just really wanted to kiss you."

Cash cleared his throat. "Ummm no, I didn't mind at all, in fact I quite enjoyed it. I was actually thinking of kissing you, but I wasn't sure how you would react."

"Well next time you won't have to wonder, since I beat you to it."

Cash couldn't have been more stunned. Julia was beautiful, smart, funny, and the more he got to know her, the more he wanted to know, and the more she seemed to be transforming before his eyes into a confident, positive person, with a zest for life, instead of the scared, rigid, distant person she'd been when he met her.

"The mountains certainly agree with you."

Julia nodded her head. "I don't know what it is. I almost feel like a different person. I feel like I'm finally experiencing what I always knew I could, I just didn't know how to access it. I feel like I'm learning more about the world around me, and more importantly about myself."

The rain had all but stopped, and by peering through the trees, Julia and Cash could tell that blue sky was beyond the storm clouds, which were moving out of the area. They took advantage of the pleasant weather, and spent the rest of the afternoon exploring the area. It was so green and lush with many streams and wildflowers. Cash picked a particularly vibrant purple flower and gave it to Julia, which she tucked behind her ear.

"I think I could build a cabin right in this spot and live quite contentedly." Julia stood in a mountain stream, the water nearly up to her knees, holding her dress up to avoid getting it wet.

"You'd build a cabin in the stream?"

"Alright, *next* to the stream. It's so peaceful here, don't you think?"

"Yes, it's wonderful, but I think when winter rolled around you might change your mind."

"Oh, that's true. I didn't think of that. Well, it would be my summer cabin then. Are the winters here harsh?"

"Yes."

Julia laughed. "That's putting it bluntly."

Cash laughed in return. "It's true, there's no two ways about it. Especially up here where we are in the mountains with the winds, and the snows. It's not peaceful and delightful unless it happens to be a clear day with no wind and you think the snow is pretty to look at."

Julia exhaled in delight. "I bet it would be beautiful to look at."

"You're beautiful to look at."

Julia smiled and swung slightly from side to side, swinging her skirts along with her. "So are you."

"I think you might be trouble Miss Julia, with a capital T."

Julia feigned a shocked look. "Who me? What did I do?"

"You're incredibly enchanting, and the worst part is that you know it."

"You better be careful then. No telling what might happen to you."

"My thoughts exactly."

Eventually they made their way back to their camp, and had dinner, while the sun dropped lower in the sky.

"Oh Cash, let's ride back up to the lake and watch the sunset."

"Alright."

The horses took them quickly there, and they settled in on the shore to watch the brilliant show the sky was displaying for them. Fortunately it was a still evening, and the water was completely calm. They had brought warmer clothing, and Cash had a blanket as well for when they went up on the divide to watch the stars.

As the sky went from fiery orange and red, to pink and purple, then finally dark, they watched the stars appear, seemingly one by one, until they completely blanketed the sky above them.

166

Cash and Julia had been sitting side by side up till this point, then Julia turned to him. "Let's hike up to the divide instead of riding."

"Are you sure? That's a lot of elevation we have to gain, and then lose again."

"I know, but we can go slow. We aren't in a rush are we?"

"No, I just want to make sure you're up for it."

"I am. I want to do this. Besides, the horses would be more comfortable here at the lake where it's peaceful. It might be windy up on top."

"Alright." Cash lit the lantern he had brought with them from camp, and held it with one hand and reached for Julia's with the other. "Let's go."

They took their time climbing, staying on the tundra and avoiding rocks they might stumble over in the dark. It was completely dark by the time they reached the top, and the breeze that greeted them had a frosty feel to it.

"Oooooo that actually feels good. I'm pretty hot from climbing."

"You'll cool off quickly though now that we're not moving. Here, let's get under the blanket."

Cash spread the blanket out on the tundra, they got on, snuggled closely together, and tucked the ends of the large blanket around them.

"This is simply astounding." Julia had her face lifted toward the sky and was enjoying the scene laid out before her.

"It is incredible." Cash was even impressed, and he had gazed at the stars in Colorado many a time. "There's just something about being up here. It's almost like we can reach out and touch them."

"Yes." Julia agreed heartily. "I'm so glad we did this. I will remember this forever."

They watched the stars for several minutes, then Cash leaned in and kissed her gently. "I've never kissed anyone on top of the Continental Divide before. I kind of like it."

"Well that's funny because I like it too, and kissing you makes this even more memorable."

"I would hope so."

"Are the stars this magnificent in Leadville?"

"Oh, they're impressive, but this is better. Star gazing on top of the divide is definitely an incredible experience. I'm glad you thought of doing it."

"I'm glad I thought of doing it too. I think it would be wrong to have traveled up here, and not taken the time to see how truly stunning the night sky is."

They stayed, huddled in the blanket, and enjoying each other's company, until the chill of where they were began to settle in.

"We better head back. Cash whispered into her hair."

Julia groaned a little. "I wish we could just freeze time and stay like this forever."

168

"If we stay, we'll actually freeze."

Julia laughed. "Oh all right." She grudgingly began to get up, and Cash gave her his hand and pulled her to a standing position.

Cash led the way with the lantern, while holding tightly to Julia's hand to make sure she didn't trip over anything on the pitch black terrain. When they reached the spot where they would descend to the lake, Cash turned and took Julia in his arms. "I really enjoyed star gazing with you. It was the most special thing I have ever done in my life."

"Oh Cash, that's adorable. I enjoyed star gazing with you too."

He leaned close to kiss her and whispered to her right before his lips met hers. "I will remember this moment forever."

Chapter 27

The next morning dawned with a certain restlessness in the weather. The chilly wind was blowing far stronger than a gentle breeze, and huge puffs of billowy clouds blew rapidly over the mountains, sometimes momentarily obscuring the tops of the peaks from sight.

Cash and Julia broke camp, and with everything securely tied down, and several layers of warm clothes on, they headed back up to the divide to continue along the Tonohutu Trail.

It was difficult to communicate due to the wind, but after a while on top, it either improved a bit, or they grew used to it, because Julia was still interested in climbing two more mountains that would be easily accessible from the divide. They struck off trail again, this time to the north so that they could climb Knobtop, which was an easy scramble up a big pile of rock. They completed it fairly quickly and Julia was happy to announce that her tally was now at four mountains climbed.

On their way back to their horses from Knobtop, Cash noticed some ominous looking clouds moving quickly toward them. "We better forego Gabletop, and get back to the trail. I don't like the looks of those clouds."

It was still fairly early in the morning, and the clouds did not look like a typical afternoon thunderstorm. They were grayish white, billowing, and enormous. The strong wind was blowing them right toward them and Cash knew in an instant that they were going to be enveloped in them soon.

"Get on your horse quickly, we've got to reach the trail before we can't see anything."

They ran the rest of the way and quickly mounted up. Cash led the way, galloping as fast as Julia, who was petrified and had never ridden a horse that fast, could keep up.

In a couple of minutes, Cash knew that there was no way they would reach the trail before the clouds reached them. The clouds had already obscured the terrain where they were headed so that Cash couldn't accurately pinpoint exactly where they needed to go.

"Hold up. We're going to be in the clouds soon. Let's go slow, and stay right next to me. Are you warm enough?"

"Yes. What are we going to do?"

At that moment the clouds swept over them, completely obstructing their view of anything more than a couple of feet away from them. Pellets of frozen precipitation began hammering them hard, and the driving wind slapped them against their faces, stinging them in the process.

"It's called graupel." Cash yelled to be heard. "It's kind of a combination of hail and snow. Let's just stop here for a minute until it blows over. Keep your head down so it doesn't pelt you in the face."

Julia nodded, but Cash could see she was absolutely terrified, and the look on her face was like a dagger to his heart.

"Here." He hopped down off his horse, and looped the reins over the neck of Julia's horse to keep them close together, then he swung up behind Julia, and covered her the best he could with his coat. "It's going to be okay. It will blow over soon."

He was thankful it wasn't a thunderstorm, because they would get soaking wet, and then freezing cold, or worse, they could be struck by lightning. The lack of visibility was definitely a problem though. Even if he thought he knew which direction he was headed, it would be so easy to get turned around or stray off course, and plummet over the side of a cliff. Thankfully they were in the middle of a very flat area, and he simply hoped he wouldn't over shoot the trail once they started moving again.

The graupel blew over in a few minutes, but the thick clouds remained. It was calmer also. The wind had died down, and now they were simply in the middle of a cloudbank which was preventing them from seeing anything.

"Are you alright?"

"Yes Cash, but what are we going to do? How are we going to find our way out of here? This stuff is thick as cotton."

"I'm going to head the direction we were going, but I'm going to angle slightly more to the right, because the trail heads that way. At some point we'll have to intersect it. You okay to ride on your own if we go slow?"

"Yes."

Cash dismounted and looked at her. "Julia." She looked at him intently. "It's going to be okay. We're going to make it out of this."

"I believe you Cash. I'm just really scared."

"I need you to be strong okay? I need you to be the woman who has climbed four mountains in the past three days."

Julia laughed a little at that. "Okay. I can do that."

Cash got back on his horse and started off slowly, with Julia right behind him. He hadn't spotted the trail before the clouds blew in, so he knew they still had a ways to go. He struggled to get his bearings, but it was impossible when there was absolutely nothing to see anywhere around him.

They rode silently for several minutes, and Cash kept hoping that at any moment they would cross the trail. Minute after minute passed though, and there was no trail, and nothing to see but white. He stopped and consulted the map. He was still confident that they were heading in the general right direction even though he had no way of actually knowing if that were true. He began to think they would have to be paralleling the trail, because he felt they should have joined up with it by now.

"What is it? What are you thinking?"

Cash showed Julia the map and pointed to where he thought they were. "See the trail runs this way, and I'm almost positive that we're heading in this general direction. I'm thinking that maybe we're paralleling the trail at this point. It could be ten feet away, but we can't see it because of the clouds."

"What should we do?"

"Let's just keep going for now. Until we run into something that tells us we went the wrong way, or something, I think we should just keep moving."

"Okay."

After a few more minutes, it was obvious that they were losing elevation. Cash consulted the map again. "I think this is a good sign. I think we've got to be here." He pointed to a place on the map. "As long as we keep heading down, and don't start traversing the terrain, I think we're headed in the right direction."

Julia exhaled a shuddery sigh and tried her best to believe that Cash knew what he was talking about.

The terrain became steeper and eventually it became obvious that they were indeed traversing instead of heading directly down. Cash stopped again to look at the map. "See, I hesitate to turn and start directly losing elevation, because if we haven't gone far enough yet, we'll get down into the woods, and then I'll really have no idea where we are."

"These clouds just need to go away so we can see!" Julia was definitely frustrated and scared, but still trying to stay strong."

"Tell you what. Let's just stop here and wait a few minutes to see if maybe these clouds will move out."

Julia nodded, and dismounted, then stood on the side of her horse away from Cash and wiped the silent tears that were falling down her cheeks. She didn't want him to see her, because she felt he'd already seen her upset far too many times since she had met him. "Dear God please give us the wisdom to get out of this." She prayed silently.

They sat side by side for a few minutes straining to see anything, and looking intently into the mass of white to see if possibly there was the outline of anything at all that would come into view.

Cash began studying an area that seemed to be a different color than the rest of what they saw, and soon he could actually see the hazy shape of something. "Look over there. The clouds are moving out."

She looked to see where Cash was pointing, and sure enough in the distance she could see the outline of some unfamiliar mountains. They watched for several minutes as slowly the clouds began to move out of the area, and they struggled to get their bearings as the overall visibility around them improved.

"It's like we fell asleep, and knew where we were, but then we woke up and we were somewhere else we'd never been before." Cash looked from the limited view of the mountains, to the map, and back to the mountains again, trying to figure out exactly where they were.

"Cash look." Julia had decided to try and see the ground that was nearby instead of focusing on what was visible in the distance. "Isn't that the trail?"

Cash looked where Julia was pointing, then took a few hesitant steps toward it. Sure enough, there was the trail, about twenty feet away from them. "Woo-hoo you found it!"

"Thank you Jesus!"

"Let's mount up and get on the trail quickly while we can in case the clouds roll back in." Cash didn't even both to put the map away, but jumped on his horse and started heading toward the trail.

In a moment they were on it, and the relief they felt was enormous. Now even if they were enveloped in the clouds once again, they would still be able to know where they were going. The trail began heading steeply downward and the terrain soon became all rock. "We found this at the perfect time." Cash called back. "It would have been impossible to be on all this rock with the horses without a trail."

"I didn't care for that experience." Julia said matter-of-factly. "I hope I never experience anything like that again. Plus it robbed me of my fifth mountain summit. We're going to have to do something about that."

"Oh are we now?" Cash was relieved that she was able to find humor in the situation. "Well we can get right on that when we get to our next camp site. We'll consult the map and find a good one."

"One that's not on the divide. I think I've had my fill of those."

"Yes ma'am. One that's not on the divide. Got it." He smiled to himself as they made their way down the trail. They'd gotten through another intense experience together, and after this one, he found himself totally in love with her. He only hoped she felt the same.

Chapter 28

Once they were down into the trees, it was as if the storm they encountered up on the divide never happened. The sky was blue, the air was calm, and it was a picture perfect day. "That's the weather in the mountains for you." Cash had commented. "It can change so fast from one thing to another, that you have to be prepared for anything."

After some discussion, they decided to head for Haynach Lakes. It was a bit out of the way, and they would have to backtrack to get back on the Tonohutu Trail after they were done there, but Cash remembered how Ben had said it was a lovely tranquil area that was definitely worth exploring. After the morning's adventures on the divide, they both decided they could use a dose of tranquil.

The ride to get there was spectacular, going through beautiful meadows surrounded by dramatically rising peaks. Julia rode with the map out, studying it and comparing it to the terrain she saw. "These mountains over here don't even have a name." She commented about some impressive looking mountains on their left. "How can that be? They're beautiful."

"Maybe they ran out of names."

"Or maybe they were just too lazy. The only named one is Nakai Peak, and we can access it from Haynach Lake when we get there."

"Oh we can, can we?"

"Well I have to climb a peak on this side of the divide, and it looks like the best option to me between here and Lulu City."

"Oh does it now?"

"Cash, you stop that!" Julia laughed heartily, and Cash was glad to hear her do so.

When they arrived at the lake, they discovered it was indeed a lovely area, dotted with ponds, and then the large main lake at the head of the valley. It was peaceful, with plenty of openness, and it was a nice level area, just inviting them to walk around and enjoy it. There were just enough trees here and there to still provide adequate shelter. Julia like it immediately.

"I changed my mind Cash. This is where I would build my cabin."

"Okay, I'll get right on that."

"Isn't it delightful?"

"Absolutely. In every sense of the word."

"Oh you!" Julia was used to his teasing, and she had to admit she enjoyed it immensely. Here was a man that was seemingly perfect in every way. He was kind, generous, caring, and she found him incredibly attractive. When she thought about the future though, her natural inclination was to retreat inside herself and shut the door to any type of relationship they might have. She hadn't any intention of falling in love when she first made plans to come to the mountains. If love was all she was after she might as well have just stayed in Boston and married one of the suitors her mother would no doubt find for her.

Still, this was completely different. An arranged marriage in Boston wouldn't be nearly as passionate as the way she felt when she was in Cash's arms. The way she felt with him couldn't be put into words. He awakened something inside her that she didn't even know existed. Was it love though? Or was he simply a tool to help her discover herself and who she was really meant to be?

She wished Sadie were here, or even Maude, so that she could get a woman's perspective on things. She liked who she was becoming out here in the wilderness. She felt stronger, both mentally and physically, and more sure of herself. She was beginning to feel there wasn't anything she couldn't accomplish once she put her mind to it.

Where she would go from here was definitely uncertain. She completely enjoyed being with Cash, but was what she felt whenever she was around him real? Would it last beyond their time together in the mountains? Could it survive everyday life in the real world?

Then she got to thinking. Everything they had been through thus far had been way more intense than everyday life. The first day she met him, he had risked his life to save hers. Then he gave up his job to make sure she and Ben were taken care of. Now he was taking his time getting to Lulu City so that he could help her achieve her goals of seeing and climbing mountains. He cared for her. He had shown that time and time again. Just this morning up on the divide when she had been so scared, she realized that even at the worst moment, she never felt totally panicked because she was with him, and she knew that he would always take care of her.

It suddenly hit her. This man was all she could ever hope for in a companion. He was more than she could ever imagine that she would ever meet anywhere, and suddenly she knew that she didn't ever want to be without him. Once they reached Lulu City she didn't want the adventure to be over. She didn't want him to go his way and she hers, although at this point, she didn't even know what way that would be.

"What are you thinking about so serious over there?" Cash had noticed her standing there, staring off into the distance at the edge of the lake.

Julia was startled, and just a bit shy at answering him, since she had been thinking of him. "Oh, I don't know, just thoughts."

"Thoughts hmm?" Cash walked toward her, then stopped just before he reached her and picked something up off the ground. "You have my heart." He said to her and opened his hand to reveal what he had picked up. It was a smooth stone that was oddly enough shaped like a heart.

"Oh Cash, that's the sweetest thing ever." Julia took the stone and inspected it, turning it over with her fingers, then she looked up at Cash and smiled as he took her into his arms.

"Thoughts huh?" He said softly to her again as he brought his forehead to hers.

"Well, yes. They were thoughts about you."

"I hope they were good ones."

"They were. I just realized that I didn't want what we have between us to end."

Cash began kissing the side of her face, then moved close to her ear. "Who said anything about it ending?" He whispered gently.

Julia closed her eyes, and enjoyed his closeness. "No one I guess, but I just wanted you to know that when we reach Lulu City, I don't want us to go our separate ways."

Cash pulled back and looked at her. "I don't think you have to worry about that. We're not going to Denver. It's a tiny mining town. I don't think we could avoid each other if we wanted to." He smiled and tucked a strand of hair behind her ear that was blowing in the breeze. "I hear what you're saying though, and you don't

181

have to worry. I meant it when I said you have my heart. I love you Julia."

Julia was in awe at his words, and realized that if he had told her that even an hour ago, she probably would have shrunk back in fear. As it was, his timing was perfect because she had decided as she stood there along the edge of Haynach Lake, that she in fact never wanted to be without him in her life.

"I love you too Cash. I can't tell you how much you mean to me. I never dreamed this would happen to me. I certainly wasn't looking for it, but somehow God knew what I needed better than I did, and he brought the most perfect man into my life."

Cash embraced her then held her close to him while he looked into her eyes and ran his fingers gently down the side of her face. "I wasn't looking for this either. I thought I would just head out and see where things took me. Well they took me to you. You're my everything Julia, and I don't ever want this to end."

"Okay now you really will have to build a cabin for me here. This is a special spot, and we'll have to visit here a lot."

"I'll get right on that." Cash joked, but then became serious. "Whatever you want, I'll do it for you. I'm yours."

Julia smiled broadly, then wrapped her arms around him and kissed him passionately.

Chapter 29

"So Nakai Peak is what we're after right?" Cash sipped coffee the next morning as he watched Julia perusing the map.

"Yes. It looks like fun doesn't it?"

"It does indeed. Do you have the route picked out?"

Cash had been teaching Julia several aspects of mountaineering during their time together in the backcountry, and was impressed with both how quickly she was picking things up, and how genuinely excited and interested she was about learning.

"I think we follow the inlet stream up to that saddle there, then turn and follow the ridge." Julia pointed to the map. "That first high point isn't Nakai, it's this point 12,052. We'll actually have to descend a bit after passing it, then regain elevation to finally summit Nakai."

Cash nodded his head in approval. "Very good. I couldn't have said it better myself."

Julia smiled, clearly pleased with both her success in map reading, and the fact that she felt Cash trusted her when it came to route finding.

"Do you want to lead today?"

"Really?"

"Of course. I think you're ready, and if you have any questions, I'll be right behind you."

"I would love to Cash."

They finished making their preparations, and set off with a small knapsack each, only taking a bit of food and water, and of course the map. The day looked to be a good one, with the sun rising in the brilliant blue sky, and only a mild breeze blowing.

The trek up to the saddle didn't take long, despite the fact that there were many boulders to clamber over. It was a rocky area, and Julia took her time, scoping out the best possible route through the rocks.

The view from the saddle opened up a whole other valley to gaze into off to the northwest. Julia immediately had the map opened up, and was identifying what she was seeing. "That lake over there must be Julian, and oh look, we can see how the Continental Divide continues on from the point where we dropped down."

Cash just sat and smiled at her as he looked at her, and how excited she was. It was as if she were totally in her element, and born to do this. The transformation that she had gone through, and the way she had gained so much knowledge about the mountains so quickly was astonishing. "Don't look now, but I think you're finding your passion."

Julia stopped staring at the mountains, and looked right at Cash. "I think you may be right. I can't explain what's happening to me, but it's like this whole new world is opening up to me, and I want to learn all I can about it."

"You've come so far, it's pretty incredible."

"Thank you Cash. I'm definitely having the time of my life."

They turned and headed southwest from the top of the saddle, to follow the ridge toward their destination. The terrain continued to be very rocky with a great deal of boulders to maneuver through. It was challenging, but fun as they pressed on, and slowly gained the top of the first hump of the ridge. "There's the summit." Julia pointed out once they could see the terrain in front of them from the top of the hump. "Oh look, the terrain is grassy. That will be nice to walk on instead of clambering over a bunch of rocks."

They continued on, following the ridge which dipped down after the first hump, then began regaining elevation. "This is it, we're almost there." Julia said on one of their stops to catch their breath.

"How many summits will this make for you now? Two or three?" Cash joked teasingly.

"At least nine or ten." Julia was quick to respond. "I snuck out and climbed a bunch more when you weren't looking."

"Oh, that must be why you're so good at it."

Julia laughed. "Yes, that is absolutely correct."

Before long they were on the summit, enjoying both the views, and their accomplishment. Cash had to admit he had never enjoyed climbing mountains as much as he did with Julia. There was just something about the connection between the two of them, and the way that they both seemed to be on the same wavelength whenever they were hiking. They shared a mutual passion for the mountains, and it brought them even closer together. He had a sudden thought, that seemed to bring together everything he had been feeling lately, and he couldn't wait to tell Julia.

"I've been thinking."

"Uh-oh, now you? Yesterday it was my turn, now it's yours." Julia smiled at him. "What's on your mind?"

"You know how you said yesterday that when we got to Lulu City, you didn't want me to go one way, and you go another?"

"Yes." She moved closer and sat down next to him on the large flat boulder he was seated on.

"Well, what if we didn't go to Lulu City?"

"What do you mean?" She searched his eyes for any sort of clue as to what he was talking about, but had no idea where he was going with this.

"I've thought a lot about what we've talked about in terms of finding your passion in life. I know that mining definitely isn't mine, it was just something I was doing while I was trying to figure out what I really wanted to do with my life."

Julia listened intently as Cash continued. "I've been watching you. You've transformed into this amazing, confident woman, who's doing all kinds

186

of things that I bet you never even guessed were possible. Whether you've fully realized it or not, you've found your passion in life. Being in the mountains agrees with you, and being with you in the mountains agrees with me."

Julia smiled and put both of her hands on either side of Cash's face. "Yes, it does agree with me, but I still have no idea what you're talking about. If we don't go to Lulu City, where do we go?"

Cash took a deep breath and continued. "I think we should go to Grand Lake. It's an actual town, kind of like Estes Park, and people go there to vacation and explore the area like they do in Estes. I think we should be mountain guides, and lead people on excursions into the mountains."

"Are you serious?" Julia was overwhelmed with the possibility, but also very excited. What Cash was saying definitely resonated within her. She knew she wanted to be with him, and she knew that she had found herself in the mountains. What an amazing thing to put the two of them together and accomplish something with her life that made her feel absolutely and totally complete.

Cash took both of her hands in his. "There's something else too." He knelt on the ground in front of her, and Julia gasped with giddy excitement. "I fell in love with you, pretty much the first moment I laid eyes on you. You are the most beautiful woman I have ever seen, and you mean absolutely everything to me. I want to

187

spend my life with you Julia. Will you marry me?"

"Yes Cash!" Julia shrieked with happiness and threw her arms around him. He picked her up and spun her around before setting her down gently.

"A marriage proposal on top of a mountain! I never would have guessed. I know where I want to take our first clients."

Cash laughed and kissed her gently.

"Oh Cash, you've made me so happy. I couldn't imagine anything more perfect."

"Waking up to you and knowing that I get to spend every day with you for the rest of my life is the most perfect thing I can imagine. I love you Julia."

"I love you too Cash."

Chapter 30/epilogue

Three weeks later a wedding was held in the town of Grand Lake, Colorado. Julia's entire family, her parents, her sisters, and their husbands were in attendance, as well as Cash's parents and his two sisters and their husbands. Julia's parents had been surprised at the news she was getting married, but upon arriving in Colorado, and meeting Cash, and then his family, they couldn't have been happier for her.

They both told her how proud they were of her for carving out her own life, and making her own decisions and choices to do with her life what would make her truly happy. Her mother was skeptical at first of Julia guiding people into the mountains, but with Cash by her side, and the vast knowledge of the area that they had been acquiring since arriving in Grand Lake, she decided it would be a very fitting profession for the two of them.

Cash's family was a little disappointed he wouldn't be returning home to run the family mine, but he and Julia both promised to visit as often as they could, and perhaps someday their hearts would be drawn in that direction.

They had been able to reach both Ben and the Cummings by telegram to let them know of both their wedding and their future plans. With winter quickly approaching in the high country though, neither would make the long trek over the divide to attend the wedding. Cash and Julia had promised to visit the following summer when they had plans to summit Longs Peak.

Julia's father gave them a substantial amount of money as a wedding present, and aside from using some of it to establish their mountaineering business, and also build themselves a house on a beautiful piece of land just outside of town, they also used a portion to establish a mission in conjunction with one of the local churches. Julia headed it up and oversaw the distribution of food or clothing or whatever the need may be to those in the area who needed extra assistance. She was glad that she finally got to do what she had intended to do from the very beginning of her journey west.

Julia's heart was full of love and appreciation for her heavenly father whom she felt had overseen every part of her journey, and had given her more than she could have ever dreamed in both Cash and their mutual love for the mountains. She would often smile to herself as she counted her numerous blessings, and would feel indeed that there was nothing more fulfilling than learning how to live.

Made in the USA
San Bernardino, CA
23 November 2014